Sister Gumbo

Sister Gumbo

Life, Sex, and More Sex

Ursula Inga Kindred and Mirranda Guerin-Williams

Brown Books — Dallas, Texas

Sister Gumbo — Life, Sex, and More Sex

Printed and bound in the United States of America

ISBN 0-9710103-0-7

For information, please contact Brown Books
16200 North Dallas Parkway, Suite 225, Dallas, Texas 75248
972-381-0009
www.brownbooks.com

Cover illustration by Sedric M. Miles

First printing 2002

Acknowledgements

We'd like to make the following acknowledgements:

God, who inspired us to write this book.

Mary Julia Quiett (Mama): Our maternal grandmother who was never at a loss for words, and who blessed us with our mother, Barbara Dean Quiett-Guerin-Harris-Hilliard.

Mother, we love you. Thank you for the sacrifices you made when we were young, and for your advice (even when we didn't listen). Thanks for always being honest and for making us laugh so much! And thanks for your encouragement.

Our husbands: Wade and Jerome—and our children; Jazmyn, Alvin, Guerin, and Justin—we love you more than you know. Thanks for your patience and support while we were interviewing, writing, rewriting, editing, re-editing, etc.

The ladies we interviewed (you know who you are). Thank you for being totally open and for sharing your stories with us. This book would not have happened without you.

Our sisters in "Suede" for all the sleepovers and talks long into the nights which also inspired this book.

The ladies at Brown Books: Milli Brown, Kathryn Grant and Suzanna Brown, for recognizing our potential and working with us so diligently.

Sedric (Montreal) Miles: our talented cousin who did the artwork for our cover illustration. Thanks for being so determined and not giving up when we were so picky.

And last but not least, all of the sisters (and brothers) of the world who have stories to share.

TABLE OF CONTENTS

MOTHER'S GUMBO

Barbara Quiett-Guerin-Harris-Hilliard

1 cup	flour
2 onions	finely chopped
1/3 cup	green peppers, finely chopped
3 cloves	garlic, minced
1 bunch	green onions, finely chopped
5 tbsp.	cooking oil
2 15-oz.	cans of tomato sauce
5 cups	water
2 lbs.	crab
2 lbs.	shrimp
1 lb.	smoked sausage

In a large pot over medium heat, sauté oil, flour, onion, green pepper, and garlic until flour browns. Add tomato sauce and water and bring to a boil. Lower heat and cook for 45 minutes. Add shrimp (deveined), crab, and sausage. Season to taste. Cook an additional 15–30 minutes. Serve over rice. Makes 12 servings.

Introduction

What could a book titled *Sister Gumbo—Life, Sex, & More Sex* possibly be about? Well let me tell you, it's a book about the **Gumbo** of women's lives!

Just as gumbo is only as good as the ingredients that go into it (the shrimp, crab, sausage, onions, garlic, spices, etc.) *Sister Gumbo* is good for the same reason. It has life ingredients, based on experiences with men, love, sex, advice, infidelity, and all the other day-to-day stuff we deal with as we go about the business of living as women.

Sister Gumbo began when we two sisters originally from Louisiana, decided to interview several of our close friends, women of all ages and walks of life, about their experiences. Once we told them of our desire to write a book and that their names and other identifying characteristics would be changed, they seemed to enjoy opening up and speaking honestly and directly. We found that most women don't mind talking about their lives as long as they know they're not being judged.

We wanted to write a fun and enjoyable book, and although there are other books already out there dealing with this subject, we feel they are often too analytical or clinical. Our desire is that each woman who reads *Sister Gumbo* will be able to reminisce, laugh, cry, agree, and maybe even disagree with these women, without having to determine *why* she lived her life the way she did, because after all, it is her life.

We hope to make light of the fact that, even though we as women sometimes make bad decisions and may not be proud of some of the things we've said, done, or endured, our individual experiences enable each of us to create our own Gumbo. We often draw from this rich stew to help another sister just when she thinks no one understands what she's going through. Hence, *Sister Gumbo—Life, Sex, & More Sex* exists to make it easier for you to feel free to tell it, even if it doesn't always feel good, because your story may help someone else.

So now that you're relaxed and ready for a good read, turn on some soft jazz, pour yourself a nice glass of wine, sit down in your favorite space with *Sister Gumbo*, and enjoy!

SELF

self (self) noun
selves (selvz) plural

The total, essential, or particular being of a person; the individual.
The essential qualities distinguishing one person from another; individuality.
One's own consciousness of one's own being or identity; the ego.

Past

Aging

Friends

"What a desire! . . . To live in peace with that word: Myself."
—Sylvia Ashton Warner, 1945

"Baby, just keep living."
—Barbara Quiett-Guerin-Harris-Hilliard

"Seldom visits make better friends."
—Mary Julia Quiett

"The best way to deal with women
is to feed them with a long-handled spoon!"
—Mary Julia Quiett

"Can't nothing make your life work if you ain't the architect."
—Terry McMillan, 1989

Past

Cheyanne, forty-something Cheyanne, my beautician for the past few years, started telling me her story at the same time she started curling my hair, and I was hoping like hell she wouldn't burn me as she'd done once before when she got to talking too much. A robust little woman with creamy, brown skin and hair that any woman would kill for, she's been doing hair, passing out advice, and telling stories for the past 15 years. She's the kind of beautician who treats your hair like it's hers, and even gets offended if you do something to it yourself. Once, when I was so bold to ask her how she found the time to keep her own hair looking so good, she replied, "Baby, I have to make time for me because don't nobody want you doing their hair if you're walking around with your head looking bad. Okay? After all, I'm a licensed cosmetologist, not a kitchen beautician."

I told her about the book and asked her to schedule my appointment for her slow day, when she could give me about two hours of her undivided attention. She obliged, asking me to come on a Monday morning and then telling me to bring her something for breakfast because she'd probably be hungry. It was a cold, January day, but by the time I got to the salon she already had it nice and warm, actually kind of cozy, and the smell of perms, shampoo, and hot curling irons lingered in the air. The radio was tuned in to her favorite station—one that played hits from the '70s and '80s, and she was putting the finishing touches on her own hair when I breezed in.

We ate breakfast and had our usual small talk before she directed me to the shampoo bowl. But because Cheyanne is such a perfectionist, she let me know in advance that I couldn't start asking questions or tape recording until I was in her chair. I for one was glad she'd suggested that we wait because a thorough shampoo was one of the things her clients anticipated on each visit.

Cheyanne rubbed, scrubbed, and gently massaged every spot on my head, and it got me so relaxed that I could've gone back to sleep. She unscrewed the huge tub of conditioner and asked, "So you want to know a little about my life, huh? Well honey, let me tell you."

"I got pregnant when I was sixteen years old by a guy who was in the army, and he was only nineteen himself. I'd met him at the army base where my stepfather was stationed, and it happened the first time we had sex, even though I didn't know that's what we were doing. I didn't even know what a penis looked like. All I know is he took it out, and I asked, 'What's that?'

"When he said, 'Nothing,' I said, 'Okay,' and I let him put it in me. I was just that naive. Of course, at 5 feet 2 inches and 95 pounds soaking wet, it wasn't long before I started showing, even though I'd tried my best to hide it. Eventually my mama came up to me, poked me in the stomach, and asked, 'You pregnant?'

" 'No ma'am,' I lied but she kept on poking and prodding like she could find out the truth if she kept poking long enough. She looked me straight in the eyes and said, 'If you pregnant, I'm gonna beat your ass.' When she left my room I cried and cried. I'd rather take a beating any day than be pregnant.

"But I was and when my mama and daddy got through screaming and calling on the Lord, Jesus Christ and everybody else in heaven, they asked me if I wanted to get married. Hell, I was sixteen years old and about to have a baby; I didn't know what I wanted. We got married when I was almost three months pregnant, moved into base housing, and fought almost every day the entire time we lived together. I was young and silly, still in high school, and running on the track team, definitely not ready to be a wife and mother, the same way he wasn't ready to be a husband and father.

"He was still chasing women and hanging out drinking with his buddies. Some of his girlfriends would even come by our house or call at all hours of the day and night. When I found out he was messing with a friend of mine, who was only fourteen, I realized he had a serious problem. I didn't blame her, but he should've known better.

"I always kept the house clean and I'd cook dinner for him every day before he came home from work, even though the only thing I wanted to eat was Jell-O and cereal. I may have only been sixteen, but I damn sure knew how to clean up a house and cook a meal. To me, it was like playing house. I'd rearrange the furniture nearly every weekend, and some days I'd clean the house before I even left for school.

"He didn't want me to hang out with my friends because he was worried that somebody would tell me what he was out there doing, so the only way I got to really talk to my friends was when I ran track. A couple of months later I'd gotten too big so I had to drop off the team and, of course, he was happy because that meant I no longer had a chance to hang out with my friends. He was always acting jealous, and I never understood why since he was the one who was always in the streets.

"It didn't take long before we both realized we were in a bad situation. I was no longer in school. Here I was, isolated from my friends and family, while he was acting like he wasn't even married, so things went from bad to worse. My parents lived about thirty minutes away by car, which meant about an hour and a half if I walked, and I did walk many a day because we had no transportation.

"Every time we had a big fight, I would take off walking to my mama's house. I think I came to know where every curve and pothole was on that route because I walked it so many times. I'd get there all upset and worn out, and if my parents were there, they'd start to fuss, reminding me once again that I shouldn't have gotten myself in that situation in the first place, and telling me a girl in my condition had no business walking that far. Then about an hour later, my husband would drag his sorry ass up there to get me, and we'd either walk back or my parents would drive us, lecturing the entire way.

"When I started my ninth month, my friends surprised me with a baby shower one Saturday afternoon. I guess I should've known something was up because he normally wouldn't let me go anywhere with them but this time he told me I could. I was so happy and excited, and it was the biggest baby shower I'd ever seen. Several of my friends worked, so they'd gotten together and bought me everything I needed; a baby bed, clothes, diapers, and toys. I must've stayed there all day, probably because I was so happy to get out of that damn house I was cleaning all the time.

"Well, baby, when I finally got home with all that stuff that my friends helped me pack in, the door hadn't even closed good behind them before he was trying to start a fight.

" 'You been gone all damn day; what you been doing?' he demanded.

"I told him, 'I've been at my baby shower. Look at all this stuff. We hardly have to buy anything.' I said all this real quick because I didn't feel like fighting.

"He acted like he didn't hear me and kept on yelling at me. 'I don't give a damn what they bought. You been gone all day long. You didn't cook before you left; now you coming in here acting like a kid with some new toys. I ought to kick your ass.'

"I knew he wasn't mad about me being gone; he was mad because he couldn't get out in the streets until he knew exactly where I was. He ranted and raved awhile longer before storming out of the house, even though he could have just left before I got back. After he left, I put everything up and went on about my business. I wasn't even upset because I was so used to this shit by now. That very next day I was looking for one of my favorite shirts and a pair of pants, and since I didn't have many maternity clothes anyway they shouldn't have been that hard to find. I soon realized that not only was that outfit missing, all of my clean maternity clothes were missing, and I had nothing left to wear except two dirty outfits in the laundry, and the clothes I had before I got pregnant. I searched all over that house and finally found my clothes hidden behind the sofa in the living room. And guess what? He'd cut them into little bitty pieces, like he was crazy or something. I was so hurt. What did he think I was supposed to wear now? When he came home, and I asked him why he'd done that, he told me he did it to keep me at home because I'd been gone too long the day before. What a damn fool."

I was starting to get a little uncomfortable because Cheyanne seemed to be reliving it all over again and taking it out on my hair. The more she talked, the faster she moved. I started to ask her how she could coordinate talking, drinking a soda, and curling my hair all at the same time, but she was on a roll and I wasn't about to be the one to interrupt. Even people calling for appointments didn't break her stride.

Cheyanne continued: "That was almost the last straw, but I was in no position to leave since I only had about three weeks before the baby was due. Honey, you won't believe what finally had to happen before I left his crazy ass.

"One Sunday night, about a week later, this movie was coming on that I really wanted to watch, and I wanted him to watch it with me since we'd been getting along okay for the past few days. The movie was coming on at 8:00 P.M., and he left at 7:00 P.M. to go get popcorn and soda. At 7:45 P.M. he still wasn't back, nor was he back at 8:00 P.M. when the movie started. I was peeping through the blinds, knowing he'd show up any minute. Two hours passed, then three, then four, until it was midnight and he still wasn't home. When I woke up the next morning and he still wasn't there, I cleaned up the house and waited for him upstairs in the bedroom because I knew he was off work that day.

"He finally made it home and came upstairs reeking of alcohol, and I asked him where he'd been. He had the nerve to get smart and tell me, 'I had a few drinks with the guys and fell asleep at the barracks. Why you questioning me?'

"Right away I knew he was looking for a fight, especially when he threw his coat across the bed like he didn't know what a hanger was, then headed back down the stairs. I picked his coat up to hang it up because I can't stand it when clothes are flung all over the place. When I picked up his coat, and his drawers and T-shirt fell out of the pocket, and I was ready to go off. I went storming down the stairs behind him, holding the drawers and T-shirt in my hand and asked him why his underwear was in his pocket if he was at the barracks with his friends all night. I was only sixteen, but I wasn't no fool.

"He was still stuck on being smart and told me, 'Girl, don't be asking me no questions; I told you where I was.'

"I took my pregnant self back upstairs and went into the bathroom to take a bath, but before I did anything else, I got the plunger and put it between me and the door, within reaching distance because I knew he was up to something. He'd tried to catch me naked once before so I couldn't leave once he started fighting with me.

"Before I could get in the tub good I heard him coming up the stairs, and when he opened the bathroom door I could tell he wanted a fight by the look on his face. He started talking shit but I didn't say anything. I just grabbed that plunger and knocked the dog shit out of him. He fell down, probably because he was still drunk as hell, and I waddled out of that bathroom, doing my best to get out of his way, but he caught me and slapped me. I fell halfway down the stairs, but I came up on my feet and ran down to the bottom and got an umbrella that was standing in the corner. When he came down after me I tried to stab that bastard's gizzard out before running outside, naked as the day I was born. The guy next door was a military policeman and he must've heard everything because he was peeking out the window at me. I was so mad I gave him the finger! My husband came out on the porch and slipped, which gave me a chance to go back in the house and lock the door. I was leaving his ass for good this time.

"That whole sorry incident caused my water to break and I went into labor two weeks early. I called an ambulance to take me to the hospital, called my mama to meet me there, and once my daughter was born and I told my daddy what had happened, he told me I was never going back to live with that fool. My ex only saw his daughter twice and that was when she was born and when she was four months old because he was too stupid and embarrassed to come around, even though he knew where we were. Here it is twenty-two years later and even though my daughter sees him from time to time, and we're still legally married, I never looked back.

"When my daughter asked me why I hadn't filed for a divorce, I told her, 'Because, as long as I'm still married, I can't make the mistake of doing something that damn stupid again.'

"And even if I had it to do all over again, I don't think I'd get married because I like to come and go as I please. I don't like to answer to nobody. Shit, I have enough trouble deciding what I want to do to make myself feel good, let alone worry about what a man wants and needs."

"You don't want to ever get married again?" I asked, when I could finally get a few words in.

"No, I'll just stick to dating. That way, I don't have to bother with cooking, cleaning, or screwing unless I want to. I can get some when I want it, then tell him to take his ass home, and that's just the way I like it."

"You're still single and still dating after all this time so let me ask you a question about that. Have you ever dated a man who wasn't black?"

Cheyanne looked at me and pursed her lips. "I'll tell you straight up. I'm not for interracial relationships. My nephew got a white girl pregnant and when I found out I was like, 'Oh hell. He's already got enough problems in this world just being a black man; now he done gone and got a white girl pregnant.' My sister had a fit. And what about the child? Society always has to put people in a box, but there is never a box that mixed children can choose. Maybe they want to check Asian and Black, but they don't have that option because they can only check one box.

"Then you get people who treat you badly because you're mixed—blacks as well as whites, because you know we can be just as prejudiced as they are. I know because I was mean to my light-skinned cousin when we were little. I was always onto her about thinking she was better than everybody else because she had light skin and bone straight hair. I didn't realize at the time that it wasn't her choice that she looked the way she did." Cheyanne shrugged her shoulders. "I'm embarrassed by it now, but I was really hateful to her. And as a child, I myself was teased about my lips. Now the tables have turned. People are paying to have shit injected into their lips to make them look like mine—and oh, by the way, they're no longer called big, they're called full. Ain't that some shit."

Miss Nora, sixty-something "My mama always said you have to love yourself before you can love other people, so I love me. I love everything about me. I believe you should always be kind to people and if there are those who are less fortunate, share whatever you have. As a matter of fact, let me show you what I've got in my deep freezer," said Miss Nora as she put down her coffee and got up from the table.

Miss Nora is a lady I've known since I was a child. She moved into the house next door to us, after divorcing her husband and leaving Arkansas with her two daughters. My sister and I often played with her girls while growing up, and since Miss Nora drove the school bus, she was off during the summers when we were out of school, so we couldn't get by with doing too much mischief. Her daughters now live out of state, but we keep in touch with her as often as possible because she's a sweet lady, and fun to be around. She kept us kids cool and happy many a summer day with her Dixie cups and homemade ice cream. When I entered her home my eyes immediately went to her kitchen counter where she used to keep a box of ice cream cones, an ice cream dipper sitting in a little bowl of clean water, and a jar full of the change she earned from selling her confections to the neighborhood children.

She noticed me looking around and commented, "You remember eating my ice cream, don't you? Well, I'm still making it, and those Dixie cups too. The only difference is I charge a little more now because I'm on a fixed income and this little change helps. I only charge 15 cents a scoop, but they like my ice cream better than what they sell in the store and it gives me something to do. You want one?"

My own grandmother used to do the same thing for the kids in her neighborhood, and as we made our way to the garage where Miss Nora had not one, but two deep freezers, I felt right at home. "Look in here baby," she said. "All these vegetables are from my garden. I've got some mustard greens, crowder peas, squash, lima beans, and black-eyed peas in this one here. My friend brought me these catfish he caught last week. I've even got a 'coon that I bought from a man down the street. See?" she tugged at the freezer bag so I could get a better view, "The feet are still on it. They have to sell them to you with the feet on so you can be sure it's a 'coon."

Why would someone want to eat raccoon, I wondered, as I tried to keep myself from imagining what else could be passed off as raccoon . . . possum . . . a large rat? The vegetables looked wonderful, but a raccoon?

"You young people don't know nothing about good food. I'll bet if I cooked this 'coon with some sweet potatoes and you didn't know what it was, you'd be licking your fingers," she laughed.

"Even though I live by myself," she continued, "I like to have food in my freezers because I came up through the Depression and going to bed on an empty stomach is no fun, even when you're on a diet. We were always taught to keep plenty of food on hand for those hard times, and I like to have extra food because I cook for my senior citizen friends who can't cook for themselves anymore. I do other things for them, too, like take them to the doctor, help them get their medicine, or go to the store for them."

We sat back down at the kitchen table. "Child, I could talk all day. I'm too old to be keeping secrets, so I don't have nothing to hide. I married a man I really cared for when I was 18, but I was never in love with him. I really liked him and he was good to me at first. But he was seven years older than me, and I just wanted to get married because that's what everybody else was doing. By the time I found out marriage wasn't everything I thought it was supposed to be, and that he was running around on me, I already had my first child. Since I didn't want my children to have different fathers, I stayed with him until I had my second one and decided I wouldn't have anymore.

"Being married was okay at first, but you know when you have a husband he expects you to have sex with him, even when you don't feel like it, and that used to get on my nerves. I didn't mind all the other stuff I had to do as a wife, but sex was a chore and he used to get really mad if I wouldn't give him what he wanted.

"Other than the sex part, I loved cooking for and taking care of a family, and since I never finished high school, I didn't work outside my home because, for number one, I didn't want nobody else raising my girls, and I never knew I was capable of doing anything else. I'm not saying there's anything wrong with staying at home though because I enjoyed it. I never worked until I divorced my first husband, but I didn't need to because he took good care of us financially. He liked to run around, but he cashed that check every week, kept a few dollars for himself, and gave the rest of it to me so I could take care of the bills.

"Now, after we had that second baby, that's when he started to change, and I guess I started to change too. I was getting tired of always being at home while he was gone on the weekends. He started to drink a lot and when he was drunk he would sometimes kick me out of bed, call me all kinds of names, and start accusing me of doing shit I wasn't doing. I'd warned him time and time again that one day I was gonna act like I'd lost my mind and just shoot him because I was getting tired of that, but he didn't believe me. Sure enough, he started that shit up one night when I was dog tired, so I jumped up, went into the other room, got my pistol, came back, and shot his ass."

Miss Nora picked up her cup of coffee, black with a single teaspoon of sugar, and calmly sipped it as if telling this story about shooting somebody was just a normal everyday occurrence. She continued with her story: "Fortunately for him, he caught the bullet in his thigh because I was aiming between his legs. We divorced after that little episode, and I got a job cleaning house and cooking for a white family. About a year later I met another man whom I married, but I didn't love him either and he used to hit me, too. He blackened my eyes, kicked, and cursed me the same way my first husband did. I don't know why some women are attracted to the same kind of man over and over again, you'd think we'd learn."

Miss Nora offered me a slice of lemon pound cake that she'd baked just that morning. Of course I wasn't going to say no because I remembered how good her pound cakes were. I was in heaven as she poured me a glass of cold milk to wash down the cake.

"I quit working because he wanted me to stay at home," said Miss Nora. "But although I enjoyed being at home during the day if my girls needed me, and I liked having a home-cooked meal ready when they got home, I wanted to get out sometimes, too. My second husband was always going out on the weekends, so one Saturday evening I told him I wanted to go out, too. He said I couldn't go with him because he was going out with his friends. So, I got a babysitter to stay with the girls and went out with my girlfriend.

"We went to a club called *Maxine's*, and I spotted him as soon as I got inside the door. He motioned for us to come to the table where he was sitting with another guy, and said, 'Hell, I didn't think you were serious, but I guess you found my ass, didn't you?'

"I didn't even respond. I was just glad to be out somewhere. Later on I got up to go to the bathroom and this woman followed me inside. She must've been drunk because she had the nerve to tell me she was dating my husband. I didn't get mad at her; I got mad at him. When I got back to my table, I told him what the woman had said and he got to cursing and carrying on like he'd lost his mind—acting like I was the one who had done something wrong. Then he started calling me names, and what did he do that for? Something went all through me because before I knew it, I'd jumped up, grabbed an empty beer bottle off the table, and started wearing his head out. He never even had a chance to get up out of his chair."

Miss Nora placed a piece of cake into her mouth and chewed. "My girlfriend was begging me to stop hitting him. She said he was going to bleed to death, that I was going to kill him, but I didn't care. I wanted to kill him. In fact I even screamed at the top of my lungs, 'Let the mother fucker die. He's called me names for the last time.' Then I threw the bottle down, picked up my purse and my drink, and got ready to leave his ass sitting there bleeding right there in that club.

"Then he started to beg, and plead with me, saying 'Baby don't leave me. I won't hurt you no more. Please take me to the hospital.'

"I was like, 'Take you to the hospital? Hell no. The only thing I'm going to do for you is go home, get my gun, and come back and kill your goddamn ass.' I don't get mad easily, but I'd taken all I was going to take. I thought my grandmama must've turned over in her grave a thousand times for all the shit I'd taken from this fool.

"I think that was the beginning of the end of that marriage because after that I went out every weekend, and he couldn't handle me being out there like he was, even though I wasn't out there with no man. I was just out having fun with my friends, but every time I went out, he'd end up jumping on me when I got back home. I tried to defend myself, but he always caught me off guard and I was tired of him hitting me.

"Even though I was always taught that you should stay with your husband no matter what, as long as he's taking care of the bills and everything, it just didn't make sense to stay with him if we were going to be fighting all the time. Those words my mama used to say, 'Always love yourself,' stayed in my head. But how could I love myself if I was staying with him and letting him beat my ass all the time? Since I knew in my heart that I didn't deserve to be treated that way, I knew it was time to go. So that's what I did.

"For the most part, I've had a good life. The only thing I regret is the foolishness I put up with when I was younger from the men I married and the men I dated. But I guess we all do that. I can say that I learned from my mistakes.

"When I was out there dating I always got a good man because I didn't go with a man who had no job and no money. That's crazy. If a man can't take care of himself, what can he do for you? See, that women's lib stuff did us some good, but it also put us in the position where we have to compete with men, and I don't like that. Men don't see women the same way anymore, and that's the reason they don't treat us like ladies.

"They've gotten so used to us taking care of ourselves that they don't know how to take care of us. Some of them don't even want to know how. It's not necessarily the way they're being raised either—it's just that some women are weak, many have low self-esteem, and since there appears to be a shortage of men, at least a certain kind of man—some women will do anything to get a man. They give them money, buy their clothes, pay their car notes and their rent. Some even let them move in rent free, and I never thought I'd see the day that things would get to that point.

"And these young men walking around with their pants hanging off their ass—what's that all about? I sure hope they don't think it looks good. Back when I was young, a man wouldn't dare dress that way, and if he did, my mama wouldn't let him in the front door. Lord, it's just unbelievable. Don't these girls understand that accepting a man who acts like he doesn't care about himself gives him permission to treat her like he doesn't care about her either?

"When I'm checking out a man the first thing I look at is how neatly he dresses and how good he smells. I like a man whose shoes are so shiny you can see your face in them, and whatever he has on, even if it's cut-offs, must be neat and clean. His body must also be clean because if I'm getting with a man and he takes off his clothes and I can smell him—and he smells bad—that knocks me away. I can't stand that! Some men will put cologne on right on top of funk, and that's a damn shame.

"I passed by one the other day who was handsome as he could be, but he reminded me of some of the men I used to ride the bus to work with back in my younger days. After wearing the same clothes all week to work, some of them would come back on Monday and get on that bus with those same dirty clothes on.

"Don't get me wrong; I don't have a boyfriend right now, but I still love men—good-looking, tall, solid men—especially one tall enough to pick me up and hold me in his arms. I love pretty teeth, a pretty complexion, and a well-groomed head of hair. And you know what? It doesn't make no difference what his skin color is to me, as long as he knows how to give me the best of everything, because I always give my best. I also think it's important that a man be grounded spiritually. Otherwise, he can't be a good leader, and I'm not interested in a man who's too worldly. I'm not talking about a fool who wants to recite scripture while we're making love or nothing crazy like that, or someone who thinks he's holier than everybody else. But I do like a man who attends church regularly and has a spiritual sense of how a man is supposed to treat a woman.

"I don't like cheap men. The men I dated knew they couldn't go to no K-Mart or Lerners to buy my clothes. I always made it clear that I don't wear cheap clothes, I don't drink cheap drinks, and I don't wear cheap perfume. Honey, after what I went through with those two husbands, I knew I'd have to set my standards high in order to be treated the way I thought I should be treated."

"So what about being in love Miss Nora?" I asked. "You said you weren't in love with either of your husbands. Have you ever been in love?"

"Baby, love is a wonderful thing, but I don't believe in making a fool of myself over it. When I was a young girl, my grandmama told me I should never love a man so much that I couldn't walk away if things got bad. She said, 'If a man loves you and cares about you, that's nice, but you can't put that in a cash register. And being in love or making love won't buy you no clothes or anything else you need. If he ain't giving you any money, he's going to give it to somebody else, so go ahead and get yours. If he's got something left to give another woman, that's fine, too.' So, being in love has never really been an issue with me. If a man is good to me and we enjoy each other, I don't think I need to fall in love or anything like that. From what I've seen, love is just too complicated anyway.

"A long time ago I used to go with this guy who was a manager at McDonalds. He always gave me money, but when it was time for my daughter's graduation from college, he didn't have much cash so he brought me some of everything that McDonald's sold. I got on the phone, called my friends, and had them call people. Child, people came over and bought all that stuff from me! Big boxes of stuff like hamburger patties, french fries, and apple pies. I had over $1,800 when I left to go to my daughter's graduation. I appreciated the fact that even though he didn't have enough money to give me, he cared enough about me to help me get it. He was good with money, but on the other hand he was very jealous.

"He got mad at me one time because I was out partying and he couldn't find me. He went to my house and took all my clothes, wigs, bras, and panties, and put them in his car. Then he took the car somewhere and parked it. Then he came back, climbed on top of my house and waited for me. When I drove up, he jumped off the roof and was holding a machete—scared me to death. He took that machete and swung it at my dog, cutting one of his legs off, and then threw him over the fence in my neighbor's back yard. When my neighbor heard all the noise and came running outside to see that dog, she almost died.

"It just goes to show you that even the good ones can get crazy. But as long as I have a choice, I'd rather have one who's crazy about me and good to me at the same time, than be with some fool who doesn't have anything and still has the nerve to try to treat me bad.

"Overall, I'd say I had a pretty good life, even though there were times I had to struggle. I had to have sex with some men who I really didn't care that much for because I had children to raise and you know how that is.

"I raised two beautiful daughters and made sure they got their college education, but they have their own lives now so I try not to bother them too much because I like being able to take care of myself. I've learned to love myself even more than I did before, so even though I do things to help other people, I also do things for myself. I decided a long time ago that it's okay to help others, as long as I help myself, too. It's okay to be good-hearted, but it's not okay to let people use you or abuse you. And you know what, it took me a long time to learn this, but I don't put anybody before God and myself, and as long as I do that, I know I'll be alright."

Sadie, fifty-something I met with Sadie in her cafe, which was appropriately named *A Cozy Little Cafe*. For the past 10 years she's owned this wonderful little place where I frequently eat lunch. She's very attractive, and nice as she can be, but when she's in her place of business, she's a professional and demands the best from those who work for her.

I've seen women throw their weight around when they're in positions of authority, but Sadie does it with such class that her staff, comprised of about 10 percent black women and 90 percent black men, in every different hue and height, seem to enjoy being ordered around by her.

A Cozy Little Cafe is the first black owned and operated upscale cafe I've ever been in. With jazz playing softly in the background and walls covered with pictures of people like Ella Fitzgerald, Count Basie, Duke Ellington, and The Original Savannah Band, I felt right at home and proud, sort of the way I'd felt when I visited Sylvia's, that famous restaurant in Atlanta.

Sadie greeted me at the door, a tradition she's kept over the years with each and every customer whenever possible. She was wearing a beautiful black suit, pearl pumps, and her usual bright smile. She hugged me and started talking to me in that fast Louisiana dialect as soon as I got inside. Sadie is a serious red-bone with short, curly, golden brown hair—*good hair*—as we often say—and beautiful light brown eyes.

"Sit down baby, and excuse the 'church clothes.' I'm only dressed this way because I had a meeting this morning and I haven't had time to change yet," she explained. "Would you like some juice or coffee?"

"I'll have some coffee, thank you," I said while admiring her attire. "I love that suit." She motioned to a waiter and told him to bring a pot of coffee, two cups, and plenty of cream and sugar, since we both drink it the same way—a little coffee with a lot of cream.

"Thank you, baby," Sadie told the waiter. "I hope you don't mind if I slip off my shoes. I like to look good, but I like to feel good, too, and right now my feet are killing me."

"Go right ahead," I replied. "I certainly know that feeling."

"So, you and your sister are writing a book, huh? What do you want me to talk about?" she asked.

"Talk about how you were raised and go from there," I suggested.

"Okay, to start with, I was the seventh of eight children, but the eighth one, a baby girl, died at birth. Since I ended up being the youngest and the last girl, after my mother had five boys in a row, I was treated a little bit special by my daddy. We were extremely close. I think he favored me over the other kids, which was wrong, but that's just the way it was, and I favored him over my mother. We were a close-knit twosome, and the boys protected me 100 percent.

"I was never allowed to date, and I was never allowed to have company like most teenage girls. Whenever I went out, I went out with my brothers to places where other teenagers went to dance. My parents owned a small cafe, so I would spend a lot of my time there because that's where they were most of the time." Sadie motioned to her surroundings. "A lot of the decor I have in here came from their place. No matter where I went, I had to get permission from both my parents, and one of my brothers would be there to take care of me and walk me back home.

"Put that over there, darling," Sadie said, winking at one of her sexy young waiters and making him blush. "I was a tomboy, so it didn't bother me to have my brothers along.

"It wasn't until my junior and senior year in high school that I realized I didn't have the freedom that other girls had. They could go out on dates and ride in cars with boys and I was never able to do that, so I had to slip out a couple of times. You know, you got out and did your little thing with the little boys, the normal teenage stuff that kids do. A couple of my girlfriends slipped out one time too many and got pregnant, which scared me to death because I loved my father so much I didn't want to take the chance of hurting him that way. Especially since my sister had gotten pregnant and had to get married at 15 years old, then had another baby by the time she was 17. By the time that baby was born, she was separated and had moved back home, but to make matters worse, she ended up getting pregnant two more times by her boyfriend! Now remember, she was separated, not divorced, and had the nerve to get pregnant by another man, twice!

"That in itself was a big thing because you just didn't do that back then, so Daddy put her out. It was terrible, just terrible, and I'll never forget the look on her face when Daddy packed her shit up and told her she had to go. Then her husband filed for divorce, so she didn't really have anywhere she could go. Mama and Daddy took custody of her two older kids to make it easier for her. Daddy said she was unfit to be a mother since she'd gotten pregnant by another man, so he didn't want her raising them anyway. I was still very young at that time, probably about 10 years old, so I grew up with her kids. She rented the house right across from ours and her boyfriend moved in with her. He was a light-skinned black man with blue eyes and blond hair. Daddy would hardly ever let her two oldest children go over to visit because he didn't like the boyfriend, so she always had to come to our house. It was a terrible thing.

"Because of what happened to her, I was scared to do anything wrong. I didn't want Daddy to think badly of me; I wanted to remain his favorite. My sister was family, but it was clear to me that she wasn't loved the way I was. Daddy would hug me and say, 'Hey, Miss Sadie, how's Daddy's baby?' But with my sister it was like, 'Hey, how you doin'? Y'all doin' okay?' He treated her like family but not like close family. They never did get close because Daddy felt that any woman who'd do something like that wasn't a good woman. Now, men could do that kind of thing all the time.

He did it himself. But quiet as it's kept, I knew Mama was a cat, too. I just kept my eyes open and my mouth shut."

Sadie noticed the head waiter trying to get her attention. "Okay, sweetheart, you can just leave those liquor receipts on my desk," she said with another flirty wink. Damn, she had a way with these men. They just grinned and bowed at her every word, and you could tell she enjoyed the flirting as much as they did.

She gave me her attention once more. "Honey, these young men are something. They love older women and I love young men. They work hard for me, and it don't cost me anything extra to be nice!

"As I was saying, Daddy was a good looking man, looked like an Indian with green eyes. He had a pocketful of money all the time and this straight black hair that he'd slick back. The women would just go crazy over him, young and old. I think he always had girlfriends but I found out that Mama had a boyfriend too, a man she'd known all her life who had been married to her best friend. I guess before this man's wife died, they'd all been good friends. His wife died at a young age, you know how some women died young back then. I guess she was like 31 or 32 at that time. Anyway, she died and Mama used to date her husband—I know this for a fact!

"I never saw them together, but I remember that whenever she'd get mad at Daddy she'd say she was walking to the bus station so she could catch the bus, and I'd watch her. The first couple of times it happened I was running and crying because I thought my mama was leaving. When I got close enough to see what was going on, I hid to watch and see if she got on the bus to leave, but there was no bus. Instead, a man whose face I couldn't make out would be there in his old coupe and they'd take off going towards town. When I saw this I figured Mama was okay and that he was probably taking her somewhere to cool off and would bring her back home later that night, but she didn't come home. She had relatives who lived about 30 miles from where we lived and she'd stay over a few days. Then Daddy would go make up with her and bring her back home. I started paying attention to this cycle so I figured out what was going on, but I'd never tell my daddy because I knew better. He would've killed her because even though he was a soft-hearted person, he was deadly if you made him mad.

"At the cafe when people were acting ugly, he'd say, 'Look here, don't do that. Just leave. Leave right now.' But when he said 'Goddamnit, I said leave!' you knew he was going to pull a gun and shoot at somebody because he was really mad when he used that word. He never cursed, so even at home, when he said 'damnit' all of us would get up from the table because we knew he was mad and things were going to get bad. Mama—and Lord knows I'm just like her—was kind of quiet, but she could curse like a damn sailor when she got the slightest bit pissed off.

"When I finished high school I moved to Los Angeles with one of my brothers. I met my husband the first month I was there. I was young and not real street smart, but I knew a good man when I saw one, so we got married five months after we met. It was wonderful for the first 15 years while I was at home raising the children, but when they got old enough to take care of themselves in the evenings, I decided to go back to school and that was a problem because my husband felt threatened.

"By the time our oldest child was in high school, I had my degree, and had given a lot of thought to opening and running my own business. But when I mentioned the idea of a cafe, he hit the roof and told me he didn't understand why I couldn't just be happy being a wife and mother. He said he'd always tried to make things comfortable so I wouldn't have to work. He couldn't understand why I wanted to start my own business.

"I'd enjoyed raising my children, but I didn't want to go through life not having achieved anything on my own and always being dependent on him. Marriage is not a guarantee for a comfortable life. The cafe was supposed to be a family business; I wanted the kids to learn how to run it so they'd have a sense of what it was like to be self-employed and make their own business decisions. It's good that we encourage our kids to go to college and get degrees, but we also need to teach them to bring some of that knowledge back to their own neighborhoods.

"I used to think this cafe would be the end of our marriage, but we've been together so long now, what's the use in either one of us starting all over again? Of course, we've had our ups and downs and both of us have done our share of wrong in this marriage, but it all came together once we both matured. After I'd been married for awhile I realized I wasn't going to find everything I was looking for in one man. That's just not possible."

"A lot of women feel that way. How did you come to that conclusion?" I asked.

"I had to look at the things that were most important to me and just deal with the rest because there is no perfect mate," Sadie replied. "I think women go into marriage thinking he'll eventually want to do everything it takes to make us happy, that he'll change in the areas we want him to change in. Usually that doesn't happen. We're not perfect, and neither are men, but we have to mature to the point where we can deal with that and learn to concentrate on their strengths rather than their weaknesses. Bitching at a man all the time won't change him, it will only make things worse, believe me.

"I'm not saying women should lower their expectations. I'm just saying that love and marriage is only what you make it. Sometimes you have to give a little more than you get, but in the long run, it will all work out, as long as you've got a decent man.

"My husband and I had our fights when we were young, but I learned from my parents that loving someone means you try to work things out. Love keeps you around and keeps you going, even through the bad times. If your man has good family values and he's a good husband and father by your standards, then you might have to put up with some shit every now and then. If you can pack up and leave when you get into a little argument and he says something like, 'You bitch too much,' then you weren't in love anyway because you'll take a lot if you love your man. You'll take an ass whipping if you know you've done something wrong. I don't care what these women are telling their girlfriends. Some of them know they've had their ass whipped and they deserved it."

I couldn't help but laugh as she stood up, put her hands on her hips, and started working her neck.

"Some women are always talking about what they will or won't do, saying shit like, 'Girl, I'd leave his ass if he even thought about hitting me. I don't have to take NO shit off NO man, and I don't know why you're staying there putting up with his shit.'

"I know better than to say what I won't do because I've taken plenty of shit from my husband and he's taken plenty from me. That's what love is all about. You know you need each other, so you don't just walk away from a relationship when you've invested your time and energy, just because you have a little spat.

"Now that I'm old enough to look back on all that, I'm glad we worked through our hard times. I think I made some good decisions and my life has turned out pretty well. I enjoyed staying home with my children for as long as I did, but I'm also happy that I stood my ground and followed my dreams because when I look around and see what I've accomplished, I can say I'm truly proud of myself."

Sadie sat back down and poured herself a fresh cup of coffee. I paused and thought for a moment. "I know this is a completely different subject, but I'm going to ask you anyway because I really want to know how you feel. You got married young so you may have never experienced this, but I'd like to know how you feel about interracial dating."

Sadie smiled and put her feet up in the chair across from me. "I did get married when I was young, but I was single for a little while too. And just because I got married young, that don't mean anything, because I'm still a woman and I still made mistakes and did things I probably shouldn't have. You know what I mean? I like men, period. I don't give a shit what color they are. I've had them as black as this suit, and I've had them as white as a damn albino. Color doesn't matter to me. What matters is that a man treats me right.

"I used to date a black man who was so sexy and so beautiful I had to pinch myself to make sure I hadn't dreamt him into being. He was a professional man and had more things going for him than he knew what to do with. He had the perfect job, the perfect house, the perfect car, and the perfect dick, but he treated me like shit and I put up with it because I was young and didn't know any better. He made it clear he wasn't the settling-down type and whenever we went out, he'd show up late, if he decided to show up at all, then he flirted with other women with me standing right there next to him.

"We were at a party one time and I'd left the room to go powder my nose or something, and when I came back he'd disappeared. I thought he'd gone to the bathroom, too, so I waited about ten minutes before I started searching for him. I stepped out front to make sure his car was still there, and then I went out back and walked around to the pool, but everyone had gone inside. As I headed back toward the house I heard this whispering and giggling coming from the pool house. Then I heard his voice.

"Well, of course I went to investigate, and what did I find? My man was groping this woman's ass with both hands, and she was kissing him like her life depended on it. He acted all embarrassed and apologetic when I cleared my throat to let him know I was standing there. Then he had the nerve to blame the woman for coming on to him! I was so through with him after that I didn't know what to do, but I had to be cool because he was driving me home.

"After that, I decided to date somebody who didn't seem so wrapped up in himself, so I started seeing this guy in one of my classes. He was white, nice looking, and pretty low key with a dry sense of humor. He'd been after me for some time, but I was worried about what my brother would say, so at first I didn't want to date him. But then after that other asshole I was dating messed up, I decided I'd try it and I must admit, he was nice to me and very thoughtful. If I even mentioned that I liked a certain book or album, he'd go out and get it. And when we went on a date, I had his undivided attention. It was like no other woman even existed when I was around him, and that was a wonderful feeling. So, I learned that color doesn't matter. All that matters is how you're being treated."

Porsche, thirty-something

When I drove up Porsche had already parked her brand new Mercedes under a huge oak tree and set up everything like she owned the damn park. I'd brought along some of my famous walnut chicken salad and some fruit because I claimed to be on a diet, but here she was sitting on a blanket with a basket full of grapes, summer sausage, crackers, two types of cheese, and two bottles of wine on ice. I should've expected that, since Porsche always lived up to her nickname, "the original material girl." She even brought some beautiful little plastic wine glasses with saucers and napkins to match, and I was happy to oblige her since it was such a pretty day.

We'd decided to meet at the park because Porsche, although very educated and proper at times, could be just as loud as she was professional, so meeting her at some nice restaurant for dinner or at a club for happy hour just wouldn't work.

As I walked up, she was grinning, satisfied with herself and her setup, and ready to talk, since she'd already had her first glass of wine. "What's up girlfriend?" "Nothing child. I was just sitting here trying to decide what all I want to tell you," she laughed. "You know I can talk."

"You sure can, and I imagine that wine won't hinder you either," I replied. "How long have you been here? Looks like you tried to start without me."

"Oh, about 30 minutes or so. I couldn't wait to get out and enjoy the sun. Isn't it beautiful out here?"

I agreed, and after spending a few minutes talking about the book idea and what was going on in our lives, Porsche cut up some of the sausage and cheese, poured herself another glass of wine, and began: "When I was about six months old, my mother gave me to my grandparents and I lived with them until an aunt and uncle of mine who were in the military returned to the States. By then I was around two, I guess, and I lived with them until I graduated from high school and went to college. My real parents did have other children who lived with them, but I was the seventh of eight children and just happened to be the one they couldn't afford to raise or some shit like that, but I'll get to that later.

"From what I understand, my father never finished fourth grade and my mother didn't finish high school, so my immediate family was relatively poor. They lived in the projects, and my sisters and brothers didn't have a lot of the things I had. On the other hand, my aunt and uncle were pretty well-off, and they gave me everything, materially, that I could ever want. But because my aunt wanted to do what she thought was right, she sent me to spend every summer with my real family, and that's where the madness began because those were the worst summers of my life.

"They never accepted me because I was different. If someone who'd never seen me before walked up and asked if I was their sister, they'd say, 'No, she ain't no kin to us. She just some girl we know.' And that really hurt my feelings. They used to call me 'baby shit yellow' and they'd make me and my younger sister compete against each other all the time. And believe it or not, my mother participated in it.

"One summer when I was seven years old and my sister was six, they asked us to spell ice, a really easy word. My sister couldn't spell it, so they asked me to, and when I did, they beat me up because I could spell ice and she couldn't. I'll never forget that.

"Another time my younger sister and I were fighting because they made us. I punched her in the nose and it started bleeding. Do you know my mother whipped me for punching her, and for winning the fight, even though she'd sat there and watched them instigate the whole thing? By this time I knew for sure they were crazy as hell, but I still didn't understand what was going on until years later when my father died.

"He wasn't around much during the summers when I was there; I had no relationship with him at all and only called him by his last name, Jackson, even though the other kids called him Daddy. But then, I called my mother by her first name, even though my sisters and brothers called her Mama, so that doesn't mean a whole lot, right?

"Well, my mother died a few years before, and when Jackson died I went to his funeral. I felt nothing for him at all, but I went back home to be with my so-called family. Everything was fine during the funeral, but afterwards when we got back to the house and there was just us kids and close friends, I was talking with three of my four sisters and one of them brought up the fact that Jackson might not be my real father. I figured that would make sense because I don't look like anyone else in my family, and the fact that they'd kept seven kids out of eight made it seem even more true. So, I asked my oldest sister and that's when the shit hit the fan. She got all upset and started crying, saying she didn't know why I would start some shit like that at a time like this. Then she had the nerve to say that every time I came home I made everyone else feel uncomfortable.

"She was screaming that I always had the best of both worlds and they never understood why I just couldn't be satisfied with that, and then accused me of being the 'golden child.' Imagine that." Porsche made a face at me.

"Still, I tried to calmly explain my perception of my family life and tell her how I always felt like I was nobody's child with no immediate family and no one to call Mom and Dad, but she just didn't want to hear it. By this time my brothers had come from outside because of all the noise. They sided with her, of course, asking, 'Why did you even come to this funeral? You weren't really our sister anyway. You lived with our aunt and uncle.' Like I'd made that choice.

"So, I cursed all of their dumb asses out, and then ran outside to try to get myself together. While I was walking around the backyard, sniffling and minding my own damn business, a very good friend of my mother's came over and started trying to calm me down.

"When she finally got me to stop crying long enough to listen, she said, 'I really wish you'd asked your mother about your father while she was alive because she told me that Jackson wasn't your father.' "

I almost dropped my cup of wine when Porsche said that. "What! You mean you had no idea at all that Jackson wasn't your father?"

"None. But wait, let me tell you how she said it happened. You know black folks can keep secrets real good when they want to. She said that my mother, two other girlfriends, and she had gone to the beach one summer in 1955 to hang out because they all had small children and needed to get away. They met a group of guys and spent the whole day drinking and partying, and one thing led to another. By the time the evening was over, a few of them ended up making out on the beach and my mother was one of them. By the time she gave me the rest of the details, I was just floored because now it all made sense.

"I asked her if she would come back in the house with me and explain this to my sisters and brothers because after all, both of our parents were dead now and there was no reason to hide the truth anymore. So she agreed and had a long talk with all of us.

"After a long silence, one of my sisters spoke up saying, 'Oh, my God. That explains it. Now we know why Daddy was always telling Mama stuff like, 'You know what you did, you know what happened,' every time they got into an argument.

"I was just numb, still trying to figure out how my mother, even though she had a hard choice to make, could just give me away rather than face up to her mistake. Even though it was very obvious that she chose to ignore what she'd done, I still did not want to believe this was the reason she'd given me away like I didn't matter at all. She chose to give me away rather than have him walk out on her.

"As I sat there, listening to everybody try to make sense of this crazy shit, I reflected back on my life with my aunt and uncle. It was okay for the most part, except that they had a daughter who hated having me around. She was several years older than me and had been their only child until I entered the picture. She was very angry with me for taking all the attention that used to be hers, and was constantly saying, 'Get away from me. I don't want you here because ever since you came you've been getting all the attention.'

"Therefore, during the school year I had to deal with this fool being jealous and a real bitch, deal with my other crazy ass family during the summer, and here I was a child who had nowhere and no one to turn to. I don't think anyone even considered how I must have felt.

"I never was told that I could address my aunt and uncle as if they were my parents because they didn't want their daughter to feel insecure. And when I was old enough to discuss my feelings with my aunt she'd say, 'Baby, we give you everything, how can you feel like you're not loved?'

"I tried to explain that having everything except somebody I could call Mom and Dad, or somebody I could call when my back was against a wall, had been hard for me. I tried telling her that never in my life had anyone said they'd be there for me, and I needed to hear that. You know, having things is nice, but that's not what makes a child feel loved. Every child needs to know someone is there for them, no matter what.

"I guess I really should be thankful because I could have been raised in the projects with my sisters and brothers who had little hope for a future because my parents weren't giving them any. But I was lucky because my aunt and uncle taught me to be strong, instilled good work ethics and morals in me, I guess, and sent me to college. They would always say, 'That which does not kill you will make you stronger.' So hell, maybe that's how I survive."

"So, did they adopt you, Porsche?" I asked, feeling sorry for her.

"No. Once I asked my aunt why they never adopted me. She said they tried, but my parents wouldn't sign the papers. Ain't that screwed up? She said that I was seven years old the last time they brought it up and she had a knock-down drag-out fight with my mother and they didn't speak for almost a year. Afterwards, she just gave up. My uncle was retired military, so I could've gotten all kinds of benefits since they were raising me anyway, but for some reason, my parents wouldn't approve of it. They didn't want me but didn't want anyone else to have me either. Ain't that some shit?

"So, I have all these little childhood memories that stay with me and I can't believe nobody saw how I was being affected. I finally realized my mother didn't care about me when she went on a weekend trip with her ladies' club one summer while I was there, and she came back with souvenirs for everybody but me. We were all excited and jumping up and down and shit when she opened her suitcase and started passing out stuff, but when she got to me she just said, 'Oh, I forgot you were even here.' "

"Damn, that's cold," I said. "That must have been hard to deal with, especially since you didn't even have anyone you could talk to about it."

"That was hard, and it was also hard to go from an upper-middle-class neighborhood to the projects every summer, because I still had all my nice clothes and they had used clothes that they had gotten through this white lady, so they used to take my stuff without even asking," Porsche recalled. "The last time I went was the summer between my tenth and eleventh grade year of high school. In the community where they lived, there was a summer youth work program where they got jobs for all the teenagers, so I got a job working with the little kids at the community center.

"We'd taken the kids to the high school football stadium to play, and there were some boys there who didn't work at the center, and my brother was with them. They were standing by some concrete bleachers and they were like, 'Hey, come over here.' Since my brother was standing over there I went. I didn't think anything of it. Well, they grabbed me and pulled me behind the bleachers and started pushing me around between themselves, talking about how they were going to find out what I was all about. I tried to get away, but one of the bigger guys grabbed me and the next thing I know, one had his hand over my mouth, one was holding me down, and the other one was taking my clothes off! I was literally about to be raped while my asshole of a brother acted as the lookout, because they had me naked all the way down to my panties. Then, all of a sudden, my brother said someone was coming, and they stopped and ran off, just laughing like it was the funniest thing they'd ever seen.

"I was scared to death, but what was worse, my own brother just stood there and did nothing. I know he would have been ready to fight if that had been one of my sisters, but I guess he didn't feel the same way towards me. After that I thought, 'This is crazy! I am not subjecting myself to this kind of cruelty.' And I decided if they didn't want me in their crazy, dysfunctional ass family, that was fine with me.

"I didn't even tell my so-called mother what had happened. Instead, I called my aunt as soon as I could sneak to the phone, and told her I was never going to spend the summer there again. I told her what had happened, and she asked to speak to my mother. About ten minutes later my mother told me to pack my shit. She said I was a lair and that I thought I was too good to stay there, so I left on the bus that night and never went back for the summer again.

"I graduated from high school two years later and went to a college as far away from home as I could, and for a while I was successful at getting away from those skeletons in my past. I got my Master's degree, got married, and completed med school, but my family didn't even come to my graduation. Actually, I only see them about every four years or so because even though they know the truth, they're still crazy as hell. They will never acknowledge me as part of the family, as if I'd want them to anyway, and I refuse to spend my whole life trying to fit in with people who want to hold a grudge for something none of us had any control over."

"So, with all that happened during your childhood and what you found out about your mom and dad, do you think that had a major impact on your decisions about marriage and having children?" I inquired.

"Oh, hell yes. I guess I always wanted to get married, but I can't say I have the best marriage in the world, and I know my childhood played a big part in my deciding not to have children. I just don't feel equipped to be a mother when I never knew what a real mother was supposed to do. I'm a damn good physician and I worked my ass off to get the education for that, but children don't require a degree, nor do they come with a handbook, so I wouldn't know how to nurture a child because that's something I never experienced.

"Besides, that's the reason there are so many screwed-up people in the world already; people have kids when they know good and damn well they don't have what it takes to be a good parent. If your parents weren't worth a damn, then they probably didn't teach you how to be a good parent either. How could they? You should just spare some poor, little, sweet child the expense of being born if you know this in advance. And choose another road in life."

"So is that what you did? Is that why you work so hard to be a good physician?"

"I thought that's what I was doing when I got married," answered Porsche. "But all I can say on that end is that I plan to get out of my marriage as soon as I can get some more things in order financially. Me and my husband just don't have anything in common anymore. I'm not in love with him, and the only reason I haven't already left is because my boyfriend isn't available. If he was single, I'd leave home tomorrow."

"Well maybe you aren't in love anymore, Porsche, but don't you care about your husband at all?"

"I used to love him, I guess, because I always thought when you loved a man you genuinely cared about him. And that's the way I used to feel. I really cared about what happened to him and I cared about his feelings. There was nothing I wouldn't do for him when we first got married, and I ended up losing myself in him.

"I used to leave love notes on his pillow, send him flowers, and write him beautiful letters and poems. But now," she paused, clicking her tongue and tossing her braids back, "I don't even buy his ass a greeting card because I can't find one that would express my true feelings. The days of me thinking he's everything I need are long gone, and not too soon either."

"What happened, if you don't mind my asking?" I questioned cautiously.

"Oh, he was a good husband at first. He used to send me flowers and buy me gifts for no reason except to say he loved me, too, and then one day it all just stopped. He started saying things like, 'With all the women out there looking for good men, you should be glad to have me,' like his ass was God's gift to women.

"He stopped helping around the house, wouldn't wash my car or help me keep it up anymore, and I even had to start paying someone else to take care of our yard. So, since he wasn't willing to do things for me, I wasn't willing to meet his needs either, and you know when you stop giving a man what he needs, all hell breaks loose."

"So, you're saying he wasn't doing the things you wanted him to do so you just cut the man off from sex?" I said in disbelief. "That's kind of harsh, don't you think?"

"Hey, I'm a woman. I want to be taken care of if I'm screwing a man. I truly don't understand why any woman would give her body to a man unless he's doing something for her. I got this cellular phone, my pager, and the down payment on my Mercedes from my boyfriend, but I do nice things for him, too, so he doesn't mind giving me gifts. Besides, after what I was going through with my husband when I met him, I let him know in advance that my shit is good, but it's not free, and I'm not giving it away just to get a good feeling.

"It baffles me when I talk to a woman who complains that her man won't even buy her a birthday gift, but then wants to screw any and every time he feels like it, just because he feels like it. I think that's just absurd and also very selfish because a man should enjoy doing things for his woman if he cares about her. And you know what else, if he doesn't give you what you want, you'd better learn to ask for it because otherwise, he might not know what you need.

"A friend of mine who'd been single for years had become accustomed to making her own mortgage payment. Even after she got married she continued to pay it until she finally woke up one day and asked her husband, 'Why don't you ever help me pay the mortgage?' Do you know what he said? 'Cause you never asked me to.' Can you believe that?

"I guess we all live and learn and some of us learn faster than others. As for me, it didn't take me long. I know I only have one life to live, and I plan on living it to the fullest and doing whatever it takes for me to be happy. If I don't, no one else will, right?"

"Yep, you got it," I answered. "Now let's move on to something else. Tell me, as honestly as you can, how you feel about interracial dating."

Porsche sat straight up. "Oh, this is one of my pet peeves," she said. "White girls are bold. They'll flirt with your man like you aren't even standing right next to him, and he'll eat up the attention like he's won the lottery or something. I'm sorry but that shit just pisses me off. What's so bad about it is, he tries to blow it off by saying some shit like, 'She wasn't even doing anything. Why you wanna act like that?' Porsche held her freshly manicured hands out and looked at them. "What I'd like to know is how his ass would act if a white man came up to me and started telling me how nice I look or how good I smell.

"And don't go to a club that white women frequent. I mean, they can be the only white face in the entire place and be just as comfortable as they please. I don't care how she looks, you can bet some brother is almost going to break his neck trying to get to her side to ask her to dance. He'll probably step over a few sisters to get there, too! I've seen the shit with my own eyes. I was at happy hour with some friends last week and none of us are bad looking women. We were all sitting around the table and these two black guys almost broke into a race to see who could make it to this white woman to ask her for a dance." Porsche shook her head with exasperation. "Now, I know for a fact that white men like black women just as much, but you won't ever see them step all over a white woman to ask a black woman for a dance. You'll never see that shit."

Now Porsche was fanning herself and frowning. "Let's move on to something else, girl, because that subject makes me hot. It's a damn shame that after all we've been through as people, we still have to deal with shit like that. It really isn't even worth talking about because it's not going to change anyway."

Marcella, forty-something Marcella, a strong Venezuelan woman, was raised in Trinidad. I love her beautiful accent. Listening to her always makes me long for the beaches and clear blue water of her childhood home. And when she speaks of her life in Trinidad, where we Americans spend millions of dollars to vacation, one can only wonder why she chose to leave such a beautiful place.

Marcella invited me to her home for the interview, and when I walked in, the first thing she did was tell me to take my shoes off and "get com-for-ta-ble." You know how people from the islands who still have that accent seem to pronounce every syllable in a word? Well, she still does that even though she's been here for over 20 years, but I find it alluring because you'd think she was born and raised right here in America, until you hear her speak.

Her place was small, spotless, and filled with many beautiful pieces she'd brought from Trinidad and other surrounding islands on her frequent visits, and she could tell you anything you wanted to know about each piece. The pride with which she spoke was obvious and again made me wonder why she chose to move to America. I silently decided that if she didn't tell me why, I would ask.

Since she commanded attention when she spoke with such a strong voice, it was hard to interrupt her once she got started. So, I sat and listened as Marcella told me about her life:

"I was born in Venezuela, South America, but we moved to Trinidad when I was six years old because my father was a school teacher and got transferred there, so even though I'm really Venezuelan all I know is Trinidad because that's where I was raised.

"My father was a heavy drinker. But back then in Trinidad when a person who was well-known got drunk, they would take him to a jail cell, leave him to let him sleep it off overnight, and then take him home. But my father died overnight when he was in jail because he had cirrhosis of the liver and didn't know it.

"That left my mother alone to raise all of us, which she did by ironing white peoples clothes to support us. There were seven of us and, oh Lord, a lot of hard times, a lot of hunger. I remember it as plain as day! Let me tell you something—we walked to school maybe a good five miles a day, back and forth. And in the evening time, when Mommy didn't get any work, when we hit our door coming back home from school we didn't know if there would be food in there for us or not. Sometimes we'd have food, sometimes we didn't, so we'd drink coffee, eat bread and go to sleep. I remember one time Mommy bought some bread because that was all she could afford, and she fed all of us and didn't eat one piece herself because she wanted us to have enough. There were times when my baby brother would sit down and suck his thumb and go to sleep hungry. He was just weak because he was so hungry.

"Things got a little better as we grew up because all of us started working. I started washing peoples clothes and baking for money, and I learned to cook by watching Mommy make bread. The railroad was really big there and we used to cook food and sell it to those guys who worked on the railroad, so that helped a bit.

"When I was 14 years old, my mother went to work one day and didn't come home that evening. I was the oldest and we were in the house hungry for a whole week, so we finally started thinking that she'd abandoned us because times were so hard. We were there by ourselves with no food, no nothing, but in Trinidad your neighbor is your friend. If they had food, we'd have food. If we had food, we shared. Everybody shared just like a little African village.

"Finally, my godmother called the police and they put an APB out on my mother. When the police finally located her, they told us that she'd been on her way back home from work and the driver of the taxi she was in fell asleep at the wheel and ran into a parked truck full of lumber. Mommy was unconscious for a whole week in the hospital. She didn't know her name and no one knew who she was or nothing, you hear me? We went to see her in the hospital and she was still unconscious. She stayed in a coma for a whole month. She had terrible head injuries, a broken jaw, and she'd lost all her teeth. It was just terrible. She was lucky she even lived. So, my godmother took care of us, but I had to quit school for a whole year because my baby brother was like nine months old. This happened maybe about six months after my father had died, so of course she had no money because a woman back then didn't work outside her home for money. Your husband took care of you; that's just the way it was.

"Then when my mommy got out of the hospital, she couldn't work and all that so I continued to wash for people and bake bread. We had a thing you call sweet bread so I would bake sweet bread and make dinners for people. We used the money I made to take care of everybody in my family. I made sure there was food cooked and everything, and the neighbors really started helping us because they felt sorry for us. We weren't hungry for the first time in months because everybody was giving us food and that was really a blessing, but we were still poor and had to struggle.

"Anyway, Mommy stayed sick for a long, long time. She didn't remember anything, and she was peeing on herself, and it was like I was the head of the house by the age of 15. Then, finally, when I was about 17 and about to finish high school, Mommy got well and things started to get better. I got my first real job as a maid, going to people's house to clean and everything, and that's also when I met my son's father. I was ignorant about sex, so I got pregnant by the time I was 19, but we didn't get married, even though my mother begged me to marry him. I didn't really love him, so I wouldn't marry him because I didn't want to spend my whole life being miserable. I'm glad I didn't marry him because he started doing some really crazy things right after I found out I was pregnant.

"I had my son and shortly after that, I was working for this American couple who were getting ready to come back to the United States. They asked me if I wanted to come, but I told them I didn't know nobody in the States, so why would I want to go there? After they explained the wonderful opportunities I'd have, I decided to go with them. I sent my son to stay with his father's mother until I could get on my feet, and I followed the couple to New York."

"Oh, so that's how you ended up in the United States," I commented.

"Oh, yeah. Otherwise I would've never left my home. Once I got there, they let me know that they no longer expected me to work for them. They were only helping me to be nice, and I was very fortunate to have them do that for me. I found a job working for another family, taking care of their children and cleaning and cooking for them. But I didn't like New York because the family I was staying with was different. I wasn't fast and I didn't use drugs or anything. I'd never even been exposed to drugs.

"Well, one day they left a whole bunch of stuff on the coffee table, and I was like, 'Why do they have all that grass and dirt on the coffee table? What is all this?' I figured they were really nasty, and girl, I vacuumed all the stuff off the table, stuff that just happened to be marijuana. I was 23 years old, and I didn't even know how marijuana looked. I thought the kids had just brought dirt in from outside and put it on the coffee table. I had never seen weeds and stuff in somebody's house like that, so I thought it was just terrible. I dusted everything off and cleaned the house and vacuumed the marijuana off the table—like maybe two pounds of it—and when they came home they had a fit.

"See, at home we did different things for fun, like go to the beach and play like kids because that's what we were, kids coming up. I didn't have all that other stuff to worry about."

"But Marcella, with all the talk about ganja and stuff, I thought everybody in the islands got high."

"A lot of people do, but my mother is very old fashioned, so we didn't know nothing. Even when I started my period, all she said was that I'd become a young lady. I was outside and had sat down to eat some soup, but when I opened my legs and saw this red stuff I thought the soup had messed my stomach up and caused me to bleed. I didn't know nothing about a period, even at sixteen years old.

"I didn't like the situation at the house where I was working so I wrote this friend of mine in Trinidad who had a brother in Rhode Island, and he said I could come there and stay, so I did and he and his wife and kids were a real nice, decent family.

"About a week after I got there, he started helping me to get information on the many schools available, and I just couldn't believe it. This country offers many opportunities and that's the reason Caribbeans, Africans, Indians, Asians, Iranians, and all these other foreigners come here and end up more educated than people born here. Americans take education for granted, but most foreigners will get here and find a way to educate every last one of their children.

"Just go to a high school graduation ceremony. You'll notice that when the awards and scholarships are being given out they can hardly pronounce the names. The majority of the children receiving scholarships are foreign. You seldom hear them call many Smiths, Joneses, or Shaquita whatevers—and when you do, it's usually for an athletic scholarship. I don't understand that, especially for black American parents because they have had to struggle so hard. You think they'd encourage their children to excel in school so they won't have it as hard as they did, but many of them don't even mention the word college until the child is a senior in high school.

"Shortly after I moved to Rhode Island, I started going to this school they call OIC, an adult educational center they have up north where you get your GED, and they help you find jobs and stuff. I had my high school diploma, but since I wasn't raised in the States, they helped me to take a few courses I needed and then I got a job through them. During that time I met this girl from Texas and we became real good friends. After about two years she told me she was going back home and asked me if I wanted to come to Texas, so I worked and saved my money and bought a ticket, and that's how I ended up in Texas. And that's where I met my ex-husband.

"I was a good wife, probably because I was taught that women are supposed to do certain things. Some women think that when they come home, cooking and cleaning is beneath them. I feel like that's part of your duty as a woman and as a wife. When you get married, those are the things you're supposed to do. That's what makes a home a home, you know what I mean? And washing—to me washing is a woman's place. That's the way I feel about it. I wouldn't want nobody else washing my clothes anyway.

"Well I married this guy and I was trying to be a good wife, but I knew it wasn't going to work out because although he was a nice person he was very jealous of my son, and I refused to put any man in front of my son. He started being verbally abusive to him because he didn't like him, and then we started getting along bad. He even started talking crazy to me, acting like he had no manners.

"He would tell me, 'Fix my plate,' and not ask me properly. So I simply would not fix his plate or do anything else he told me to do because I was his wife, not his servant, and I refused to let him treat me otherwise.

"I ended up hating him because he beat my son when he was six years old. It was a terrible, tragic thing and I left him because I'd rather be homeless than with some man who doesn't like my child.

"See, what happened was there was this car in our driveway and my child always liked to play by himself inside the car. I was gone to work and my husband worked nights, so he told my son to stay inside while he slept. But when my husband woke up my child was outside in the car playing with his toys. I understand that he should not have gone outside because he'd told him not to. But he was only a six-year-old child. I didn't mind him spanking my child, I really didn't, but he beat him with the buckle of his belt, and I don't think that was necessary.

"I didn't know what had happened right away, but at night I'd usually bathe him. I'd leave him in the tub and then go back and wash his back and make sure he'd washed himself because he was a little child. When I went back in there this night and I saw all these marks and bruises, girl, listen to me, I went dumb. I literally—I swear to God—I had no voice. It was completely gone. Completely. I got so mad that it was like I went into a coma for a few moments. When I finally came to my senses later that night, I packed our stuff. I did not give him a chance to explain because you don't do that. You do not hit a child like that, I'm sorry. And what made it even worse was that he was such a sweet child, he didn't even tell me what happened. Honey, he had marks on the back, the legs, the hands, the sides, everywhere. Everywhere, do you hear me? How could I lay down with my husband again after that? I couldn't. And I know what the consequences would have been if I had stayed with him. I'm sure he would have done it again.

"I had no family here and it was a good thing because if I'd had someone here who could take care of my child, I would have given him up for adoption and then killed that damn crazy ass man. That way, when they took me to jail, my son would've been taken care of by my family."

"You really would have done that?"

"I seriously would have because I was so angry I couldn't see any other solution," Marcella replied. "But then I decided that fool wasn't worth me spending the rest of my life in jail over, so I just left before he had a chance to do it again. You know, I hate him still to this day, and he's the reason I never re-married. I just couldn't bear the thought of being with someone who would do something like that again, so I've been single ever since."

"Okay then," I said in an attempt to switch gears. "Since we're talking about men and you're already fired up, I'd like to know your thoughts on interracial dating. Are you for it or against it?"

"I think interracial relationships are fine, but it's not for me. I told my son years ago that if he wanted to go that way, fine, but I wouldn't feel comfortable with it because every time I watch *Roots*, I get sick to my stomach.

"The only problem I see with it is that black women are being shortchanged because there aren't enough black men to go around as it is. Take the high school prom, for instance. When it's time for a young black girl to go to her prom, there aren't enough guys to choose from but the white girls will have more than their share because they can pick from the white guys and most of the black guys, too. It happens all the time. Then we have the cases where a black man is lucky enough to finally make some decent money, and nine times out of ten what does he do? Go get himself a white woman.

"I know people have the right to choose as they like, but if a black man wants a white woman just to be able to tell somebody he's got a white woman, who cares?" Marcella arched her eyebrows and shrugged one shoulder as she adjusted her bra strap. "Now, if that man sincerely loves that woman, he doesn't care how she looks, doesn't care how big or little she is, and he just loves her for who she is and not for the color of her skin, I don't have a problem with that.

"The same thing goes for the woman. If she really likes a man because he's nice to her and they have a good relationship, then no matter what anybody says, if that's who she wants to be with then that's who she needs to be with. I'm forty-something years old and I've never been in an interracial relationship. But if I met a white man who treated me the way I want to be treated, and if I liked him—not because he was white, but because feelings were there—I wouldn't care what color he was.

"Really, black people are still color struck from back in the days of slavery. My son is fair-skinned, but he likes dark-skinned women. As far as he's concerned, the darker the better. But if he'd married a white girl that would have been fine with me as long as she treated him right. His stupid-ass father, on the other hand, doesn't feel that way. When my son sent his dad some pictures of him and his fiancee, you know what his dad called me and said? He said, 'I don't mind him getting married to a black woman, but does she have to be that black?' I can't believe that we as people still feel that way, and all I could do was just shake my head."

"Wait. He's black too, right?" I asked. "And he's trying to be prejudiced against someone else who's black just because she has dark skin?"

"Yes, probably because he is very, very light-skinned. But, honey, let me tell you, that dark-skinned daughter-in-law of mine is treating my son like the King of Egypt, do you hear me? She treats him much better than his light-skinned father ever thought about treating me."

Eboni, forty-something Eboni's living room looked like something out of the *Architectural Digest*. It was spotless and perfectly decorated with taupe leather sofas covered with oversized pillows. Authentic pieces of African woodwork and black art were strategically placed throughout the room. On her dining room wall there was a beautiful rug made from Kente cloth and straw. She'd purchased it during her honeymoon on the Ivory Coast. Even the lamps and tables looked like they were made especially to go with her other furniture.

Although the furniture was obviously too large for the small condo she'd recently moved into, it had probably fit perfectly well in the half-million-dollar home she'd left a year ago.

I complimented her on how beautiful and cozy her place was. She forced a smile and said, "Oh, thank you. I guess it'll do. Would you like something to drink?"

Since she was newly divorced, I guess cozy wasn't in her vocabulary at that time, and because she seemed a little down, she wasn't her usual bubbly self. I knew about the divorce, but this had been her second marriage, and even though the divorce had been final for the past six months, it seemed as if she was still dwelling on it.

I didn't press the issue or ask any questions about what had happened. I figured that would come up once she loosened up. Instead, I let her talk about her childhood and teenage years, hoping that reminiscing on better days would help her to reclaim something she felt she'd lost.

"Okay, Eboni, tell me how you grew up. What kind of life did you have as a kid?" I prompted.

"I was the oldest child, and I had a good childhood because I got everything I wanted," she began. "I was the only child for six years and when they had a second baby, my brother, I was very jealous. I couldn't stand the fact that he was getting any attention because I wanted it all. One day, when he was about a year old, I walked him outside and put him in an ant bed, thinking the ants would take him down into the hole. But child, when those ants started biting him and he started screaming and hollering, my mama and daddy came running outside and my daddy whipped my ass all the way back to the house while my mama was trying her best to get those ants off my brother. I thought they were being mean to me because all I wanted was to be their only child. I really didn't think I'd done anything wrong.

"Now, I loved my mama, but I was really close to my daddy. Even though he made it obvious that he hadn't wanted a daughter, I learned to make him happy by trying to do anything a boy could do because I felt that way I could win his heart. He was a big black man with a beautiful smile that I adored, so I learned to cut the yard, climb trees, whatever, just so I could see that smile. But then he came to expect me to do these things, which kind of bothered me because it was making me tough. When I became a teenager, he got mad at me one day and said, 'You should've been a boy 'cause you're always out to get what you want.' And that didn't make sense because he'd made me that way.

"Now, as a grown woman, when I feel like I've been used, I retaliate because of the hard time he gave me. My mama gave me love, but Daddy taught me how to think like a man because he was really hard on me. If I fell down and skinned my knees and started crying he would say, 'What you cryin' for? Cryin' don't help nothing. Get up and clean your face and quit actin' like a baby.' And I would do it. One time I fell off my bicycle and broke my arm, and he threatened to whip me if I didn't learn how to ride without falling off.

"My grandparents lived in East Texas in the country, and me and my brother went down there every summer to visit. I must admit, now that I'm grown, that it was a beautiful place. But as a kid, we were bored because there was nothing to do but sit out on the front porch and wave at the few neighbors who passed by or go swimming in our cut-off shorts and T-shirts with our cousins."

"So, your grandparents had a swimming pool down in the country?" I asked.

"Child, no. They had what you call a tank. We swam in it, but they also stocked catfish and perch in there and we actually ate them. Whenever we wanted some fresh fish we'd just take our cane poles and go catch some for Big Mama to clean and fry, and you talk about good eating. I think that was the best fish I've ever eaten.

"They also had chickens and hogs and stuff, and one summer when we were down there and had just come back from swimming in the tank, my grandpa and daddy were catching chickens for dinner. We stood there and watched while they caught those chickens and wrung their necks. Then my daddy told me to catch one after it slipped by him, so I ran after it and caught it, but I was scared to death. I held it out in front of me for one of my cousins to take it, but my daddy said, 'Gal, go on and wring that chicken's neck. I know you ain't scared of a little old chicken.' Of course, I couldn't show that I really was scared, so I had to do what I was told."

As Eboni sat there, sipping on a glass of brandy, I could tell she was back in the country all over again.

"Even today when I think about it I want to cry. I closed my hands around that chicken's neck and I could feel the softness of its feathers and the warmth of its body. I started swinging it around, like Daddy and Grandpa had done, but I guess I was swinging it around too slow and Daddy thought I was playing, so he hit me on the shoulder with his razor strap and told me to quit playing. I wanted to cry so bad, but instead I closed my eyes and started swinging the chicken around faster and faster. It seems like I swung it around forever until I heard my daddy finally tell me to let it go. When I opened my eyes, the chicken's head was in my hands." Eboni looked straight through me. "You just don't know how that felt. I've always tried to put that out of my mind, but every time I have to cut up a chicken, it takes me right back to my grandpa's farm, standing in the yard with all that blood on my hands.

"The things Daddy taught me made me strong, but that also made it hard for me to show affection because he didn't show much affection towards me. I feel affectionate, but it's just hard for me to show it. I knew my daddy loved me because he spent a lot of time with me and taught me things about life. But I never felt like I had his unconditional love, and I was always trying to prove myself to him so he wouldn't think I was weak."

"You said he wanted a son when you were born, but did he ever tell you why he was being so hard on you? Especially since you were a girl?" I asked.

"No. You know how it was when we were coming up. Our parents didn't feel they needed to explain anything like that to us," Eboni recalled. "They were the parents and we were the kids, so we just did as we were told. We lived on the rough side of town, so I guess Daddy wanted me to learn how to stand up for myself. Besides, I had to be my brother's protector because he was always running his big mouth and getting into something, and I had to fight for him.

"One time he was fighting this boy and the boy put a sleep hold on him. That's when you put pressure on a certain part of a person's body and make them pass out. Well, I thought the boy had killed my brother and I got scared. I was scared and mad because I knew I had to go home, but I couldn't go home without my brother. So, I picked up a brick and hit the boy in the head and his parents ran out in the street and threatened to file an assault charge on me. When my brother came around and I took him home and told Daddy what had happened, all Daddy said was, 'Did you kick that boy's ass who was messing with your brother?' I said, 'Yes sir.' And he said, 'Well, you done damn good.'

"As I started to mature, I also started filling out. I'd never been heavy because I was such a tomboy and was so active, but I never gave any thought to the fact that one day I would have breasts and hips, let alone a butt that was so well shaped it could stop traffic. Well, one day when I was about 13, a boy, who I'd secretly liked, squeezed my butt as I was passing him in the hall. I turned around and swung at him so hard that I almost fell down, but I missed. Then I got so mad I wanted to cry, but it wasn't because he was laughing at me, it was because when he touched me I had this funny feeling inside that I'd never felt before. I didn't understand what was going on with my body, so I just cursed him and walked away.

"When I got home that day and started to change clothes, I looked in the mirror at my reflection and there I was, a young lady. I had changed without even noticing it myself, and then I really did start crying. My mama heard me, so when she came into my room and I told her about what had happened at school, she just laughed and took it as an opportunity to explain the facts of life. From that day on, I struggled with my femininity because on the one hand I wanted to be tough, but on the other hand I began to look at boys differently. I really started to like them.

"I began to talk to boys more, as friends at first, and by my freshman year in high school I had my first boyfriend who convinced me to try out for cheerleader. Of course my parents didn't feel I was old enough for a boyfriend, and they let me know right away that being a cheerleader did not mean I was going to be allowed to hang out at school or anyplace else unless I was practicing or cheering. As my daddy put it, 'Just go ahead and tell all them little hard-headed, slick-ass boys that being a cheerleader don't mean you can take company or date or anything else, so they won't make the mistake of knocking on my door.'

"Boys came by anyway, but we had to act like we were buddies and I had to act rough so my daddy wouldn't think anything was going on. If a boy wanted to kiss me, he'd pay my little brother, who was always conveniently nearby, to go around the corner for a few minutes and be the lookout while we were kissing. Really, the only time I got to do any socializing other than at school was when I went skating on Saturday evenings. That's where I would get to be with my 'so-called' boyfriend, but even then my parents would pick me up at seven o'clock."

"Seven o'clock?" I asked. "Girl, that's when the fun begins. How did you deal with that?"

"Oh, I was determined to have my fun, so I started sneaking and doing things. I started lying about where I had to go so I could be with my boyfriend, and baby, I was screwing every chance I got. They didn't really let me go on a date where a boy could come to the house and pick me up until I was a senior in high school, but by then I'd already figured out how to do what I wanted to, even with an early curfew, so my first date wasn't even exciting.

"But that first real date is when I got pregnant because I was 17 and thought I knew what I was doing—trying to use that damn withdrawal method. I figured that shit must be for white folks because it's almost impossible to get a 17-year-old black boy to stop in the heat of the moment. Of course, my parents were devastated and from that point on, I felt like I had to prove myself to everybody. Here I was, a straight-A student, a cheerleader, my daddy's heart, and I'd made the worst mistake I thought I could make. All I could think about when I found out was that Daddy had told me over and over again, 'Don't be out there making mistakes with your life 'cause mistakes are for weak people.' "

"Did you feel like being weak had caused you to slip and make the mistake of getting pregnant?"

"Really I've never seen myself as weak. Even thought I got pregnant, I finished high school before my baby was born. But I still hadn't learned anything because I compounded the situation by getting pregnant a second time when my son was about 13 months old, and I thought my daddy would die for sure. He talked about me so bad that I thought I'd never get over it. But again, it only made me stronger."

"So, did all those things you learned from your dad help you as a single mom raising two boys?"

"Well, of course it helped, but being a single mom wasn't hard for me because for the first five or six years my mama kept my kids while I worked. Being single wasn't the problem. My low self-esteem was the problem, and that's how I ended up marrying the first man I thought I was in love with. He was a wonderful lover, but the marriage only lasted about two years because we fought all the time and it was just wearing me out. Sometimes I felt like I had to be his mother, like I was raising another child. I had to nag all the time just to get him to do anything, except have sex of course. And I felt like I had to constantly pump up his ego, which was draining me.

"I think a man should be confident enough to know who he is without a woman having to constantly praise him. The funny thing is, when I met him, I thought he was very self-sufficient and that attracted me to him. But then he started acting like he couldn't do anything unless I told him to. Then when I did he'd say I was bitching, so I couldn't win either way. I guess I should have realized that good sex alone wouldn't make a marriage work.

"After we divorced, I stayed single for many years, often dating men who gave me money or bought me things that I thought would make me feel good about myself. I guess I was looking for the one man who could make me feel special, just like every woman does. But I was going through the men as fast as I was spending their money, and sometimes I'd have two visitors in the same day, which made me feel like I was turning tricks. I was trying so hard to find someone who really loved my kids and who would be able to give them the things I felt they needed. You know, when you have your children out of wedlock, you want them to be better than *regular* people, so I thought if I had a man with money, my kids could have all the things that regular people had, and then they wouldn't have to be ashamed of having a mother with no husband.

"I finally ended up falling in love with a man who did have money. He had his own trucking company. But I soon found out his company was just a front for the drug business he was running, and like a fool I married him anyway. The next thing I knew, he had me flying across the country to pick up drugs and money, and I was living a life I never dreamed I could get accustomed to. I still can't believe I did some stupid shit like that, but I was just crazy in love with him. What else can I say?

"With two Mercedes in the driveway, a beautiful home, and both of my boys driving their own cars to school, everybody was happy. Even when the boys finished high school and left the house, my husband and I were still very much in love. What I felt for him was totally different from what I'd felt for any other man.

"He took me to some of the most beautiful places I've ever seen, bought me furs and anything I wanted, and after 12 years together I still couldn't stop smiling when I was on his arm. I couldn't wait for him to come home in the evenings so we could spend time together, and even when he worked late, I'd still have his dinner waiting for him. Making love with him was a feeling I can't even express or try to explain because it was so unique from what I'd ever experienced. Just being in his presence made me happy."

She paused, trying to gather herself for what she was about to say, and I waited, afraid to say anything that would make her change her mind. The rumor was that her husband had just packed all his things and left her one night, but no one knew why. When she finally found her voice again she had tears in her eyes.

"He came to me and said he had fallen in love with my first cousin, and that they'd been having an affair for the last two years."

You could hear a pin drop in the silence that surrounded us.

"See," she said very quietly, "I loved him so much that I didn't even notice he wasn't loving me back the same way. I wasn't paying attention to the fact that he was late on the same nights every week—he'd always had meetings on Tuesday, Thursday, and Saturday evenings. So, I just thought he was doing what he always did. I hadn't even wanted to question why we made love less frequently. I attributed it to him being tired and getting older. And even though at some point I thought he could be having an affair, I guess I didn't really want to confirm it because then I'd have to make a decision, and what decision do you make when you love someone so much? I figured if he loved me like I loved him and something was going on that it would pass. Hell, I guess I was just in love and in denial and he knew it, so he took my love for granted."

"Well Eboni, since you loved him so much, why didn't you guys try to work things out?" I asked cautiously.

"When he told me what was going on, he didn't even ask me how I felt or what I wanted to do. As a matter of fact, he'd already filed for the divorce when he told me the truth, and our house was up for sale the next day. I wasn't working, so he had complete control of our finances and I didn't know what to do. Shit, I didn't even know where the money was anymore because he gave me money whenever I asked for it and took care of everything else himself.

"I could've gone to the police about his business, but then I would have implicated myself and they would have seized everything, so my ass was stuck and I knew it. I just had to take the cash he gave me, which was substantial enough to help me get my life together, and move on from there. I had no options.

"So, here I am starting all over again. It's hard but I'm trying to learn to be happy with myself and with my life. I realize now that what I thought I needed to make me complete was to be in love and have a husband and a life full of stuff. But I'm finding that true happiness comes from within and you should learn to be happy with yourself whether you're in love or in a relationship or not."

"Do you think you'll fall in love and get married again?" I asked. "Or do you even want to?"

"I'm not knocking love and marriage because I'm a true romantic. My parents stayed together, and even though I'm sure they had their problems, they kept it to themselves and they never disrespected each other. At least not in front of us. They were a team and that's the one thing I was never able to accomplish in my marriages, but I still think marriage can be good.

"Even if I never get married again, that's okay. I'm having a lot of fun dating and as long as I'm happy, that's fine with me."

"Hmm, interesting," I paused and then asked, "is there anything you would do differently if you could go back and change things?"

Eboni laughed, "Baby, if I could turn back the hands of time there are a lot of things I'd do differently. The main thing is I wouldn't have been so crazy about money." She pointed towards the Kente cloth wall hanging. "That rug cost $2,000. I saw it, wanted it, so I got it. *For The Love of*

Money was my theme song because when I was growing up, it didn't take me long to realize that when a person had money, they had power.

(Tap, tap, tap, tap, tap, tap, tap, tap, tap, tap, tap.) Eboni ran a sculpted nail along the neck of one of the wooden giraffes situated on her mahogany coffee table.

"Remember how I dressed when we were in school? Everything I wore was name brand and if I happened to be wearing orange, you could believe I'd have the accessories to match. I liked expensive things and as I grew up, I realized the only way I could keep getting these things was to have money.

"When I was in the fourth or fifth grade, I noticed that the women who looked good and wore fancy clothes got all kinds of attention. I always loved and craved attention, still do, and I always dreamed of growing up and dressing in fine clothes and driving fancy cars. I used to pick this plant we called Elephant Wings because it had these huge green leaves." She pushed her fingers through her freshly cut hair. "I'd get a bobby pin and pin that plant in my hair and pretend it was a hat. My daddy smoked Livera cigars and they had paper rings around them, so I pretended those were my rings and I put one on every finger. I'd turn my bicycle over, place a chair behind it and sit there in that chair with a sheet pulled up around my shoulders and act like I was driving. The sheet was my mink coat and the chair and bicycle my car. All my friends would laugh when they saw me doing that, but I didn't care because I knew one day I'd have those things.

"I'd ignore the teasing and tell them, 'Y'all keep on laughing, but one day I'm going to show all y'all.'" Eboni motioned to her surroundings, the expensive furniture and fine art. "When I drove up to my high school class reunion in a white Mercedes Benz, wearing a designer dress they couldn't even dream about being able to afford, and I had diamonds on both hands. Those same people who laughed at me so long ago were there to witness it, and believe me, they weren't laughing anymore. It was all a part of believing I could have what I wanted."

She reached for her empty glass. "I wish I hadn't been so materialistic, but it's a hard habit to break. I'm almost 50 years old and just now realizing there's more to life than whose name is on your shoe or what kind of car you drive. I've never been one to work a nine-to-five job because I always had a man in my life to take care of me." She looked around for the brandy bottle and poured herself another glass after offering me one.

"Now that I'm older, the men are coming few and far between and I know this figure can only last so long, but I got bills that still need to be paid. I got a part time job for the first time a few weeks ago, but it didn't last because when it came time to take my lunch break, I took an hour and a half. That's how long it takes me to go out to lunch. I have never had to limit how long it takes me to eat. Now I've got to go out there and try to find another job when I really don't even want one, so yeah, I have some regrets about some of the things I've done. I damn sure wish I would've invested some of the money that came through my hands rather than spending it all on clothes, shoes, jewels, and furs. It's hard to go from getting everything you want without lifting a finger to having to work for a living. That easy money life, that's a hard habit to break."

Kat, thirty-something "If you want a story about a sister who's got a dysfunctional relationship with her mama, you should just go ahead and use this one," Kat said. Maybe somebody else will read it and get some help because I sure as hell can't seem to make sense of it. I know I've bitched and moaned about it before, but I just don't know what I can do to make my mama happy.

"As you know, we used to be more friends than mother and daughter until I got serious with Tim and then married him. He treats me like a princess, and she can't stand that. The other day while she was at our apartment, I asked him to get me a drink of water and she made this face, looked me up and down and said, 'Lazy, lazy girl. Why can't you get your ass up and get your own water?' Like I don't deserve to be treated nice by my own husband. I just can't do anything right in her eyes, but I'm sorry if she lost her best friend when I got married. I guess I can't be her best friend and her daughter, too. It just doesn't work. And I shouldn't have to choose between her and my husband anyway."

"Hold on girl," I said. "Let me go get us some coffee and teacakes. Maybe that will help to calm you down a bit."

"Oh, okay," she said, realizing she'd started talking before we even sat down. Then she reached for her purse and pulled out several lipstick samples and placed them on the table. Kat was regal and had full, sexy lips like her mother, and she was always trying on some new shade of lipstick, trying to bring even more attention to them.

She had been upset when she called me earlier that day, almost in tears, and asked if we could meet at the local coffee house after work. I didn't really feel like doing anything except going home and relaxing with some hot chocolate and a good book because it was an ugly, cold, rainy day. But Kat needed to vent because her mother had pissed her off again, and she didn't want to discuss it with her husband because she didn't want him to know how she really felt about her mother. You know how it is—there are some things you don't tell your husband because later, he might wash your face with it.

So, I agreed to be her sounding board, and she agreed that she'd let me bring my recorder so I could take some notes for the book. Once I was there, I was happy I'd come. It was such a nice place to sit and talk because the atmosphere was so calming. It smelled of fresh coffee and baked goodies, and they always kept a fire burning in the big fireplace during the winter, which made it feel really cozy. We chose a spot close by where we could feel the heat from the fire without getting too hot. Since they had open mike scheduled for eight that evening, most of the crowd wouldn't start showing up for at least another two hours. I figured maybe Kat would be okay by then.

Kat's mother, who's from Jamaica, raised Kat and her three sisters alone after their half-French, half-black father walked out on them. Kat was only seven at the time, but she was the oldest. Her mother came to depend on her more than she should have, and continued to do so even after Kat was married and trying her best to change their relationship into a healthy one.

Even though her mother had no formal education, she always pressed Kat to go to college and get a degree so she could ensure herself a stable financial future. But lately, she seemed to be more concerned about her own future than she was about Kat's, and it made Kat angry because her mother had always been so domineering that she was afraid to confront her. I'd tried several times to get Kat to tell her mother how she felt, but she said the mere thought of that made her shudder.

So, knowing all that in advance, I was basically there to listen because I knew that's what she needed.

"Okay, girlfriend, here's your coffee," I said, eyeballing the lipstick spread out all over the table. "And I don't know how you plan to try on lipstick, drink coffee, and eat teacakes all at the same time." She just looked at me like she didn't even hear what I was saying and started talking again, while trying on the first new shade and looking in her hand mirror.

"You know, I was the only girl in my building to finish high school without getting pregnant. I finished college like Mama wanted me to, and now I'm working on my Master's degree. When I tell her that I'm getting mostly A's and B's she says, 'Well, the courses must not be that difficult,' like I'm not smart enough to make those kinds of grades.

"That's not the end of it either. I used to give her a hundred dollars a pay period just to help her out. But last week I didn't have it because I had some bills I had to pay and you know what she said? 'Well, I'll just loan you what you usually give me, and you can pay me back later.' Now, here I am putting my relationship with my husband in jeopardy because I'm giving her money behind his back, and she's acting like I actually have to give it to her.

"My three sisters don't give her shit, and the youngest one has done everything she was big enough to do, but still, she's my mama's favorite. She's had two kids out of wedlock, has never been married, dates married men, and talks to Mama any way she wants to. But you know what Mama told me and my other sisters? She said she's leaving everything to my baby sister because she needs all the help she can get!

"Here I am running over to her house every Sunday afternoon to balance her checkbook, and going to the grocery store for her every Wednesday. One of my other sisters cooks for her, but she doesn't give her any money. And the other one cleans the house, but she's leaving everything to the one person who won't do shit for her." Kat looked like she was fed up.

"Girl, she's just talking, because that don't even make sense," I said, trying to keep my thoughts to myself. Kat kept right on talking.

"But that's okay because I'm learning. Sometimes when the phone rings and I see her name on my caller ID, I don't even answer it because I don't feel like hearing her shit. My two other sisters won't do that. She has them on a guilt trip. They'll see that it's her calling, take a deep breath, and answer the phone, knowing that whatever it is she has to say might leave them in tears. I'm not doing that shit no more. I finally decided that I'm not dealing with her unless I want to. My sisters say I shouldn't do that because it could be an emergency. But if it is, she needs to call 911 anyway because there's nothing I can do. Hell, I'm not a doctor."

"Damn, I'm glad you're starting to stand your ground, Kat," I said in a surprised tone. "What made you speak up for yourself?"

"All the shit that happened last month when she accused me of being part of something I had nothing to do with. See, Mama and the sister right under me are co-owners of a house. Well, my sister and her husband are in the middle of a divorce, but she was going to let him rent the house so they wouldn't have to worry about finding another tenant. Well, my baby sister happened to drive by there and sees this strange woman with a moving van in front of the house, so she immediately went running to Mama, swearing that my sister's ex-husband was letting a woman move in there with him.

"The other woman just happens to be his sister, and not a girlfriend at all, but Mama wants to kick him out of the house anyway, just to be mean. My sister doesn't want him to have to move because it makes this whole divorce thing easier on their son, who's going to stay with his father. Well, Mama found out my sister discussed it with me and got mad and said I'm the one behind all this shit when I didn't even have anything to do with it. So, I decided to go over to her house and talk to her about it, and she cursed out me and everybody else within hearing distance. I just walked off and went outside where my baby sister was standing, looking like a damn fool with a fake-ass weave down to her shoulders, picking at her too-long, fake nails. I told her silly ass off for starting this whole mess, but I couldn't say everything I wanted to say because I ended up crying.

"Well, weeks went by and my mama didn't even pick up the phone to call me. I finally got my nerve up to go over to the house to check on her, but when I opened the door with my key and walked on in, she jumped when she saw me, like she was startled. I know she was just faking because that woman can hear a rat piss on cotton. After she got through acting all surprised, she peered over her glasses at me and said, 'Oh, it's you. You finally decided to come on by and check on me, huh?'

"She didn't even offer an apology for cursing me out. But come to think of it, I've never heard her apologize to anybody after she's been mean to them. Then she said, 'Well, I need you to balance my checkbook and pick up a few groceries for me,' as if all this shit had never happened."

"Has she always been that way?" I asked reluctantly.

"Yeah. She's never been an affectionate woman because she didn't receive any affection when she was a child. Her own mother died during childbirth. Then she was raped when she was a young girl and raised by her grandmother who had no arms. Both arms had to be amputated for some reason when she was a child, so she never received any affection and doesn't know how to show any. She often says, 'I've seen y'all hug other people, but y'all never hug me.' and I feel bad because I do hug other people all the time. But we hardly touched each other in my house when I was growing up, so I can't bring myself to hug my own mama.

"It may sound mean for me to say this, but if there's anyone I don't want to be like, it's her. And I hope I don't treat my children that way when and if I have any because this is the kind of shit that screws people up."

"So I gather you still haven't really confronted her about how she treats you when you do so much for her, huh? Kat, you've got to learn to speak up for yourself, girl. I mean, if you can't speak up to your own mama, who else are you going to let walk all over you? You can't go through life letting people treat you that way, and just because she's your mama doesn't mean she has the right to either. I hate to see you all upset and everything, but as I've told you before, this is a situation that's not going to change unless you change it. Maybe if you sit down and tell her how you feel, she'll surprise you and tell you a few things that could help you understand where she's coming from with all that drama."

"You know what? You're right," Kat replied. "And I'm not going to dwell on this situation with her anymore. I'm not even going to visit her unless I feel like it. I'll call her once or twice a week, and if she calls me and asks why I haven't been over, I'll just tell her I've been busy or something. I know that's not the whole truth, and maybe not the solution to the problem, but I do have my own life. I have a husband, a career, and other things to do besides run to her house and get my feelings hurt. So, I'm not doing it anymore. If she doesn't care about me any more than that, I'll just have to care for myself."

"Now, let's talk about something else because life is too short to focus on other people's misery. Even if that person is your mother."

With that settled, we began to talk about the other things going on in Kat's life—the positive things like her new job, her new husband, and her newly found desire to get into real estate part-time. I smiled while listening to her talk and decided that maybe this time she really would get past her mother and move to the next level of being a woman. As I'd told her many times, if she was strong enough to survive all of her mama's drama, she was strong enough to make better choices for herself. She just needed to look inside and use what she already had.

Bianca, thirty-something I couldn't wait to get to *Emel's*, the dinner club where I was meeting Bianca. It had been a long, busy day at work. I was starving, and I always looked forward to ordering their blackened cajun shrimp salad, so this interview came at an ideal time for me.

Since it was still early, barely 4:00 P.M., the place was still fairly empty and quiet when I arrived. Emel's has several cozy little nooks and crannies you can hide in if you're looking for a little privacy, and it would be awhile before the evening crowd started showing up.

As soon as I was seated and had ordered my drink, Bianca showed up looking all chic. I just don't understand why this girl doesn't have men falling all over her. She's a single, professional woman in her 30s, has no children, and has a wonderful personality. She recently moved into her own custom-built home and drives a beautiful Land Rover. But she says that's part of the problem. She says the only kind of guys she seems to meet are the wrong kind. Either they have nothing and want a sugar mama, or they feel intimidated because they think she has too much and doesn't need a man.

"Hey, beautiful," she said, as she walked into the room with that gorgeous hair flying behind her. "I'm sorry I'm late, but you know how that traffic can be."

"Girl, I just barely got here myself, so you're fine. You look so pretty. Where in the world are you coming from in those cute boots and that short skirt? I wish I could wear something like that."

"The mall, girl," she replied. "You know Foley's is having a Red Apple Sale, and I couldn't miss it. I worked through lunch and then left early so I could beat the crowd, and I'll probably go over to the club for a little while when we finish, so I had to be dressed for the occasion. Did you already order something to drink?"

"Yeah, I'm having my favorite—rum and Coke, and I've already told the waiter what I want to eat because I'm starving! He'll be right back with my drink so you can order, but then I'll ask him to leave us alone after we get our food so we can talk. Isn't this place nice?"

"Very nice," she agreed. "This would be a good place to have dinner with a date."

Bianca started talking as soon as our drinks came. She was telling me so much so fast I had to interrupt and tell her we should just go ahead and start before the food came, so we did:

"Okay, you know I'm from Pasadena, California, and I was an only child. My mother didn't work outside our home when I was a kid, and my dad was an engineer for an architectural company, so he traveled a lot. Therefore my mother and I were very close because we were always together. She made friends with a few of our neighbors, but I can't recall her ever really being close with anyone besides me. When Dad was home, he was either working on his next project, watching TV, or sleeping, so he didn't spend much time with me or with my mother, and I used to feel sorry for her because she seemed so lonely at times.

"Mother kept me busy with dance lessons and modeling classes because she grew up poor and always said she wanted to make sure I was 'well rounded,' but to me most of that stuff was boring. Our weekends were full of dance recitals and plays and stuff like that, and she was happy as long as we were running around all weekend. I felt she was trying to keep herself occupied because, without me being involved in these things, she didn't really have a life.

"As soon as I started middle school, I told her I didn't want to take ballet anymore. I was tired of going to recitals and I just wanted to hang out in the neighborhood and be with my friends on weekends. So she let me stop, and then enrolled me in African dance at the local black arts school where all the black girls went, and I loved it."

"So, you and your mom hung out all the time . . . and where was your dad on the weekends?" I asked. "He wasn't traveling that much, was he?"

"Okay, let me just get this part out so you'll understand all about my hard-working dad. When I was about 17 years old, I found out my dad had another woman and another daughter in Denver, Colorado, and the other daughter was already 10 when I found out.

"Girl, it was a trip the way it happened, because the woman actually came to our door when he was away on business, and told my mother everything. We were sitting down, getting ready to eat dinner one evening when the doorbell rang and I went to answer it. There was this little white woman who looked like she *used to be* attractive with a little girl, who looked like she was mixed, standing there looking pitiful. She asked for my mother, and I told her I'd go get her, and she said, 'Tell her that her husband's other wife is at the door,' just like that.

"My mother was acting all calm and cool. But I was like, 'What does she mean his *other* wife?' I was ready to kick her ass just for ringing the doorbell, but my mother gently grabbed my hand and squeezed it, indicating that she had the situation under control.

"She invited the woman in and offered her some dinner, and let her sit there and cry and tell her little sob story. But Mother kept a straight face and ate her dinner the entire time. Then, when the woman got through, my mother put her fork down, looked right in her face and smiled and said, 'Honey, I already knew all that shit you just told me. This ain't no surprise.'

" 'I know who you are and where you're from. I know what day that baby was born, and I know your address and just about everything else about you. But you know what? I know what my last name is too, and I know that I live in this nice house, I don't work, and I ain't gonna work unless I feel like it. And even though my husband might've been stupid enough to have an affair with you, he's not fool enough to divorce me and move in with you permanently because he knows that if he does, I'm taking his ass to the bank.'

" 'I'm taking this house, half of his current income, half of his retirement, and all of his dreams because he should have thought about who he married before he went out there and got you pregnant. I'm from the old school, you see? As long as my husband is taking care of me and my child financially, and I'm living easy without having to worry about anything, I don't really give a damn what he does when he's supposedly working all over the country.'

" 'So even though I feel a little bit sorry for you, I can't help you because you knew he was married in the first place. I am not about to conspire with you to run down a black man, especially when that black man is my husband. And as far as I'm concerned, we never had this conversation.'

"Then my mother politely walked the woman to the front door while patting her on the back, and told her everything would be alright, while I sat there in awe of her.

"Here I was, thinking my mother was a proper little lady who just didn't want to make waves, when she had already planned our future without so much as lifting a finger. I'll tell you, that really taught me how much strength a black woman can have.

"I wanted her to whip the woman's ass for even having the audacity to come to our house. You know, white women are bold! But she made me swear that I'd keep this to myself, and I felt like if she could be that patient and that strong, so could I.

"About five years ago, she finally filed for divorce. I guess she got tired of the game she'd had to play for so many years. She moved to Phoenix and bought a nice little condo and a brand new Lexus with Dad's money," Bianca laughed. "She also has a boyfriend who's ten years younger than she and he just adores her. She's happier than I've ever seen her."

"But what about you, Bianca? Are you happy? Don't you want to get married someday?"

"I'm happy, and yeah, I do want to get married. The only problem is the pool of eligible men out there seems to be getting smaller and smaller, so I can't find Mr. Right. I just broke up with Thomas after eight months because, although he was nice, he said I make him feel inferior. You remember that surprise birthday party I gave him? Well, I set it up and paid for everything because he said he'd never had a birthday party in his life. I felt like we'd been together long enough, and I thought it would be a really nice birthday gift.

"But that fool grinned and stuck his chest out all night, then when it was over and everybody left he told me he didn't appreciate me trying to make his friends think I was his 'sugar mama.' I was like, 'sugar mama? Hell, I'm only a year and a half older then you in the first damn place, so how could I be your sugar mama? I don't have to try to impress your friends; I just threw a party for you because I thought that's what you wanted.'

"Needless to say, we couldn't keep it together after that. I hate to feel like I have to change who I am just so a man can accept what I have. That's so stupid. So, now I'm on the prowl again, girl."

"Have you ever been even close to marriage? I mean, you're so pretty and outgoing and everything," I said. "I know some guy out there wanted you to be his wife."

Bianca sighed heavily. "I was engaged when I was 22, and I broke it off even though I was still very much in love with the guy. I will probably always love him. See, when we first got together, if I wanted to go somewhere with my friends, he didn't have a problem with it. As soon as he put a ring on my finger it was like he'd placed a noose around my neck. He didn't want me out of his sight, and I couldn't go anywhere without him. He began acting like he owned me, but I was young and I wasn't about to let him put shackles on me.

"Finally, I'd had enough. I told him that I refused to be locked in a cage, and I broke up with him." Bianca turned her eyes towards mine. "That's when I found out how crazy he was because he tried to kill both of us. He left that night, but he wouldn't stop calling me all that next day. 'I just want to talk to you,' he kept saying. At first I was hanging up on him, but because I wanted to see him badly, too, I finally said okay and agreed to let him come over that night. When he got there we sat and talked for a while, and I told him the relationship just needed to be over. He said maybe we could both relax if we went for a drive, and since it was getting late, I thought if I'd just ride with him for a little while he'd calm down. But once we got on the freeway he headed out to an area that wasn't very busy and started pressing down on the gas. He was making the car go so fast that it started shaking and I was really getting scared, but I didn't want to let it show. Finally, he said, 'You really gonna break off this engagement?'

" 'Yes.' I told him. 'I love you, but I can't stand being with somebody who's always acting so jealous.'

"Then he got this crazy look in his eyes and said, 'Okay. Do you see that bridge we're headed towards? If you don't change your mind by the time we get to it, I'm going to drive right off of it and kill us both.'

"I didn't believe him, and even though he wasn't slowing down, I just laughed and said, 'No you're not; you're not going to kill yourself.' He said, 'Watch me,' and pressed that gas pedal all the way to the floor. At that point, I got really scared and told him, 'Okay, okay. I'll marry you! Please don't do this!' He stepped on the brakes, barely missing the on-ramp to the bridge.

"That ride back to my house was the longest ride I've ever had. When he finally pulled in my driveway and stopped, I jumped out of the car and screamed, 'You stupid, dumb motherfucker! I don't ever want to see you again!' Then I ran into the house. But before I could get inside and lock the door, he caught me. The next thing I knew he had closed and locked the door and had his hands around my neck, and was choking the shit out of me."

"Girl, no! That fool tried to kill you?"

"Hell, I don't know what he was trying to do, but I remember seeing stars and then it started to get dark. When he realized he was really choking me he stopped and started shaking me. All I could do was try to catch my breath and get my voice back and when I did, I told him to leave or I was calling the police. He did, I guess because he was scared, and I still called the police anyway because I wanted to make sure that crazy motherfucker didn't come anywhere near me again.

"Since then I've met and dated lots of guys. Some of them I really cared about, but I haven't been in love with anyone like I loved him since that happened. I guess I'm scared because sometimes men put on one face when they're trying to get you, and then when you fall for them they show their true colors. I don't intend to end up dead or in some dead-end relationship just because I'm in a hurry to get married. I'll just have to be patient until the right one comes along."

Bianca looked at me like she had more to say. "Is that it? Aren't you going to ask me anything else?"

"Of course, girl," I replied. " That's just the beginning. The next thing I was going to ask you, since you don't mind telling me about your life, is what you would have done differently if you could do it all over again."

"If I could do things differently, I wouldn't have become sexually active at such an early age." She tried to tug her short skirt down so the waiter wouldn't trip and drop the drinks he was carrying because he was so busy staring. "I started having sex when I was sixteen and haven't stopped since. Matter of fact, it's been one of my favorite pastimes in life. Unfortunately, when I was sixteen I didn't do any of the things I should've done to protect myself, so by the time I was seventeen, I got pregnant. This was during the late '70s and my mother had always been very open with me about a lot of things, but she wasn't open enough to say, "When you think you want to start having sex, come talk to me. Maybe there's something we can do." She probably felt like she might have been condoning it if she'd offered to take me to the doctor to put me on birth control."

Bianca grimaced. "I was very thin as a teenager because I'd been dancing since I was a little girl. When you're in dance, you don't even think about gaining any extra weight. Because I was so slender I was able to hide my pregnancy for four months, almost to the point where it was too late to have an abortion. When my mother found out about it, she asked, even though it was a year too late, why I hadn't used any birth control. But since she hadn't discussed birth control with me, I wasn't aware of all the options out there."

Bianca had ordered some of *Emel's* famous hot wings, and she bit into one before she continued talking. "I was in this career enhancement program in high school, so I went to school half a day and worked as a receptionist at this small insurance company the other half. One day I was at work in the bathroom crying, and my supervisor, a black lady, came in and asked, 'How far along are you, Bianca?' She was the kind of woman you could tell anything to, so I felt comfortable telling her the truth. I was so amazed that this woman who barely even knew me could see what kind of trouble I was in right off the bat. I told her about my pregnancy and how I had kept it a secret from my mother. I cried even harder when she said I had to tell my parents because they needed to know what was going on.

"That same day I went home and told my mother. Of course, my dad was out of town. I can remember the exact day and time I told her. She was in the kitchen cooking my favorite meal—chicken fried steak with gravy, mashed potatoes, and green peas. She was seasoning the steak with salt and pepper when I walked into the kitchen and was about to roll it in flour when I told her. I just blurted it out, 'Mother, I'm pregnant.' She dropped the bag of flour on the floor, it burst, and flour went everywhere. She ignored the mess and turned off the skillet that had just begun to heat with oil, and looked at me, devastated. She had that '*What did I do wrong?*' look in her eyes. After all, she was a stay-at-home mom and had enrolled me in dance and music lessons, and took me to plays and museums to make sure I got a well-rounded education. This wasn't supposed to happen to us. Her whole face froze as she sat down, and her hands began to tremble. Then she was talking to herself, saying she didn't understand how she hadn't seen the signs.

"She bought me a pack of Kotex every month and she knew I'd been using them because the empty packages always ended up in the trash. But all along, I'd been wrapping the unused Kotex in tissue and throwing them in the trash."

Bianca caught the waiter as he was passing by and asked for more ranch dressing for the hot wings. "After my mother got over the initial shock of my pregnancy she said just as bluntly as I'd announced it, 'You don't need a child. What in the world are you going to do with a baby? You're only seventeen years old, blah, blah, blah.' I knew I didn't need a child and that I wasn't willing to put my life on hold to raise one, but my decision to go ahead and have an abortion was based on her telling me straight out, 'I am not going to help you raise a baby, so you do what you have to do.'

"The abortion was expensive because I was so far along. It cost almost $600, and my mother had to borrow the money from a great aunt so no one else would find out. I don't know what excuse she gave my aunt. I just know she didn't want to take the money out of the family account because she was afraid my dad would get suspicious.

"A week later we went to a clinic in Dallas and they did a sonogram and then gave me a local anesthetic. By that time I was 20 weeks along but the technician wouldn't tell me whether it was a boy or a girl. All she asked was, 'Where in the world is your baby? You don't even look like you're pregnant!' I'll never forget lying on that table because at 20 weeks, I knew my child was fully developed. The whole time I was there, a Lionel Richie tape was playing—the one that had *Penny Lover* on it. To this very day, whenever I hear that song, I have to hold back tears.

"It wasn't long after I had the abortion that my mother asked me if I thought I should go on the pill. It was a year too late, but at least she'd finally asked me. When I didn't say no like she clearly wanted me to, I think she was hurt. It was like I hadn't learned my lesson. She thought I chose to take the pill because I wanted to continue having sex. But in reality, I was choosing not to get caught up in another situation where I might have to abort another baby."

Bianca offered me the last hot wing. "I guess what I'm telling you is this; If I had to do it all over again, I would've waited. Because once a girl has sex for the first time and enjoys it, it's too easy to say yes to the next guy you really care about. Even when you know it's a dead-end relationship and sex won't make it any better."

Aging

Celeste, fifty-something "When I think about getting older, sometimes I laugh at myself. A little while back, my sister was telling me that when you get older, you can't hold your urine like you used to, and now those days are here for me. You know, when women have children it causes stress on the body, and as you get older your bladder and everything drops. Things are just not as firm and tight as they used to be. When I have to go, I have to go. Sometimes I cough too hard and almost wet myself. You just can't control it. I look at myself in the mirror and I see wrinkles that I didn't have a few years ago. My eyesight and my teeth are not like they used to be. And my weight used to be much easier to control, so I'm reminded everyday that I'm getting older.

"About five years ago, I'd just finished taking a bath and was drying myself off, and I caught a glimpse of my pubic hair in the mirror. One side was just about totally gray and the other side wasn't. I thought I was seeing things. You also find that your pubic hair gets thinner as you get older. One morning I looked down there and wondered, 'Where is all my hair going? Am I just losing myself?' I looked in the bed and in the bathtub. I didn't know what was going on! It seems like it was just gone overnight.

"My memory used to be excellent, but now I find myself making more notes because I can't remember as quickly as I used to. I tried to go to someone's house the other night and turned up into the church parking lot, thinking it was a street," Celeste laughed. "But I don't feel bad about growing older as long as I grow old gracefully. I'm even getting more mature with my age, and there are still many things that I want to learn. I'm just trying to stay positive about it. What else can I do?

"I looked in the mirror the other day and said to myself, 'Girl, just look at your fat stomach. You need to go sit your little fat ass down!'

"Then I got so tickled that I really did have to sit down."

Ruby, forty-something "I ain't too much into this growing older shit. The first time I noticed a gray hair I almost had a fit because it was not on my head, it was on my twat. You should've seen how fast I ran and got the tweezers and plucked it out. No more than a few weeks later it had come back, and I've been religiously plucking it out along with the two or three that have appeared in my head. What I want to know is why those hairs seem to stick out straighter than all of the rest of the hairs in my head. They just stick out there like they're trying to get attention. I swear, I'll brush my hair back and that one gray strand will stick clean out all by itself.

"I'd thought it was funny when a few years ago my cousin told me how she'd sit back in her bathroom, hand mirror in one hand, tweezers in the other and pluck out gray hairs. Now she says she don't worry about that shit no more. She said she can finally understand why some men walk around with shorts and dress socks on—they just don't give a damn about what anybody thinks, and it's a pretty good feeling.

"I also don't like the fact that it's hard for me to lose weight as I get older. I don't eat anymore than I did when I was in my 20s and I swear I must gain a pound a week. I mean, it's not like I don't watch what I eat and I'm forever at the gym, but let me go without working out for two days and I'll gain two pounds. I remember how I could eat Oreos and drink chocolate milk everyday for lunch and could still slip into some size 5 jeans. But hell, those days are gone.

"And did anyone tell you that as you get older you get varicose veins or fine hairs on your breasts, not to mention on your top lip? Well, the shit happens. I remember being a child and going over to my friend's house to walk to school with her. I couldn't have been more than nine years old at the time. Well my friend's mother bent down to give her a kiss and her gown kinda fell open, and I could've sworn that her breasts were twisted. Now I realize she just had stretch marks.

"I used to take my breasts for granted. At a size 36D, full and standing up as perky and proud as they could be, they would've given those silicone things a run for their money any day. Even when I laid down they stood up. I thought that was just the way breasts worked. Now when I lay down, they almost lay down before the rest of my body."

Jazz, forty-something "Getting older is kind of scary to me because I don't know what to expect. It's harder to lose weight, so you attract a different kind of man. Then the men that you're attracted to may not be attracted to you because you're older now and you don't have that young, hourglass figure.

"Now, don't get me wrong. There are men who appreciate my being a 'woman' and not a teenager, but I'm just not sure I can learn to appreciate it. I find myself looking at my kids lately and thinking about how I used to have so much energy. They want to be in the streets all weekend, at the mall and everything, but I can't go all day like I used to. My ass is tired, literally.

"I used to be able to screw a man's brains out and not even breathe hard, even if he was about to pass out. Now I've got to drink some wine and try to relax just to get wet because I don't really even feel like screwing at all most of the time.

"I noticed some girls in the grocery store the other day and their legs were so firm. They didn't have no cellulite, stretch marks, varicose veins, or anything. I looked at them and wondered, 'Did I ever have legs like that, and if so, can they ever look that way again?' That's scary for me, so I don't think I'm ready to get old yet; I really don't. I do look forward to seeing my kids grow up and achieve things, but I don't look forward to getting old.

"See, right now I can still put on something sexy, put on a little make-up and the right perfume, and go out dancing, and I might be attractive to somebody. I know it shouldn't matter what men think. But what normal woman doesn't want to be attractive? But as I get older I'm not going to have as many men looking at me, and the ones who do will be old just like my ass is old, right? Shit, I don't want no old man, even if I am old.

"Sometimes when I go to a place where there are a lot of young people, like at the mall, I notice that all of them are looking at each other, but none of them really look at me. It's almost like I'm not even there. I feel invisible, like I'm in a part of the world where I'm not important anymore. These young girls are so cute with their hip-hugger shorts and halter tops—no stomach at all and firm breasts. And here I am all covered up so my stretch marks and cellulite won't show, wondering why no one even looks my way. I guess I just thought I'd always be young. I never dreamed I'd have to hang out with old ass people—people older than myself—to continue to feel that way."

Kiana, forty-something "I think the one realization is that as I get older, the closer I get to the inevitable. Other than that, getting older makes me realize that as I'm getting older so are my parents and their parents. I need to attempt to enjoy their company more. I don't think I'm tired because I've gotten older; I'm tired because I'm worn out. When I saw that first gray hair I just thought, ooh, a gray hair. I couldn't believe it. I was like, 'Let me call my Mama.' "

Louise, sixty-something "I don't feel too bad about aging. When I was young it scared me because I felt that it would be terrible to deteriorate and get old and ugly, but I think that as you get older you realize that time's gonna change you. You're gonna get older and you can't stop it, but it's okay because everybody else in your life is getting older, too. I see it as a challenge to be the best looking one out of all the folks my age.

"The physical changes bother you more than anything. You look at yourself getting wrinkles and your butt getting wrinkled and your breasts sagging and white hair on your coochie. You don't feel like you're as appealing as you used to be, but you shouldn't worry about that because your husband is not as appealing either. You're both getting old together. Of course, you will have to accept the fact that it will take longer for your husband to get hard, and then he won't stay hard very long because that's just the way it is for most men.

"I think the saddest part about aging in marriage is watching a man lose his ability to get an erection because when that happens, something inside him dies. It's like he doesn't feel complete anymore. I can't speak for everyone, but that's what happened when my husband turned 60, and I was only 53 at that time. Now, when I wake up in the middle of the night and feel like I want to have sex, I go to the bathroom, pee, do what I have to do to give myself an orgasm, and go back to bed.

"Since he can't make love anymore, he drinks himself into a stupor every night so I'll think he's just not interested. But we both know the real reason he drinks like he does is because he's frustrated at the situation. I guess he thinks I must be getting it from somewhere else because anytime I'm late coming home he asks me where I've been.

" 'Out screwing,' I reply. 'Where else would I be?' Of course, I'd only say that to lighten up the situation, but I know he wonders if it's true."

Shantay, thirty-something "Just like my little throw pillow reads, 'THE BEST IS YET TO COME.' As long as I'm able to come and go when I want to and not have all those aches, pains, and cellulite on my thighs, I'm looking forward to getting older. At least that means I'm not dead."

Porsche, thirty-something "I like growing older! I'm more in control of what I choose to do with my life and I feel like I'm growing old gracefully. I'll be 40 soon and I'll stand up against any 27-year-old any day because I got it going on, you know what I mean?! When I look at myself in the mirror I don't see an old woman. I feel really good about how I've managed to take care of myself through the years.

"I've still got firm, perky breasts. I figure that since we put lotion on our legs and arms, we should take care of our breasts the same way, so I put firming cream on my breasts. You know that stuff you use to keep the cellulite down? I put that on my breasts every single day and judging by the compliments I get from my boyfriend, it must work. I was with him the other day and I was wearing these thong panties and he said, 'Porsche, do you realize you'll be 40 soon?'

"I asked him if *he* knew I'd be 40 soon, then I pulled my thong aside to give him a view of my almost 40-year-old stuff!

"I had my tummy done a few years ago, and I'm happy with the results so I'm thinking about getting my breasts lifted next. I mean, why not? People who want to build a house save money for it. I ain't building no house, so I can save my money and spend it on myself because that's what's important to me."

Giovanni, forty-something "Girl, let me tell you something about getting older," said Giovanni. "My titties are sagging, my stomach is hanging, and I hate that shit. I don't understand why gravity has to be so cruel.

"The other day while I was sitting in the bathtub, I remembered why I'd come to prefer showers. My damn stomach has gotten so fat, it felt like I was sitting in an inner tube. Ain't that some shit? I used to be so fine, I could get just about any man I wanted. Then I got married, got comfortable, and had these kids, and all hell broke loose. It's almost like somebody took my body and gave me another one while I was sleeping one night, because I certainly didn't realize I was looking like this. This body just snuck up on me.

"There's this fine, young nigga' at work who flirts with me all the time. He's 23 years old, stands about 6 foot 3 inches, and weighs about 180 pounds, and I can just look at his ass and imagine screwing him all night. But, hell, I'm so damn tired I can't even keep my husband happy, so what am I gonna do with him? He keeps telling me he loves older women, but young men also like to change positions all the damn time when they have sex, and I'm too old to be doing all that shit. I wouldn't want him to catch a glimpse of my breasts hanging down in the mirror while he's working it from the back, so I ain't even trying to mess with him because I'd be too embarrassed to look at him the next day.

"I guess that's just life. You either get old or get dead, and I'll have to admit I'm not quite ready to be dead."

Friends

Miss Charsie, fifty-something "I had a friend who was very dear to me. We'd known each other since first grade. She called me one day and said her husband had left her, and she needed me to co-sign a note to help her get a loan. It wasn't a big deal for me, especially since I knew it would help her out, because I knew she'd help me if I needed it.

"I signed that note and ended up having to go to court and pay CASH for whatever it was she'd bought with that money because she never made one damn payment.

"I paid an attorney to locate her, but he wasn't able to find her because all he had was her social security number and she was never one to work. I just couldn't believe she'd do me that way because she was my lifelong friend.

"I haven't heard from her since. She just took the money and left. I don't even know if the story she told me about her husband leaving her was true. She could have gone off with him for all I know. That's low, isn't it? Really low. And I thought we were tight. So, since that happened, I don't sign for anyone, no matter who they are."

Giovanni, forty-something "My best friend is a really sweet guy who I used to be very much in love with. I still love him. I mean, we still love each other, but we're both married. So after three years of meeting at every Motel 6 in town, we decided that we should do the right thing and leave the sex out of our relationship because we were becoming very possessive of each other. Besides that, I got tired of asking for a room in the back.

"The reason I can truly say he's my best friend is because he's been there for me through thick and thin. We can talk about God, marriage, children, sex, money, politics, and even though we may not agree on everything, we respect each other's opinions.

"I remember one time we got into a heated discussion about religion. I was looking for a church to join and he suggested I visit his church with my family. Well, that didn't sit well with me because I'm not trying to be friends with his wife, and his pastor is a straight up ho and everybody in town knows it. You talk about the blind leading the blind. I don't even know why they're following the man and paying their tithes at that church because most of it's probably being used to take care of all his women.

"I tried to get my friend to understand that I know we don't worship the pastor and that I'm not perfect, myself. I even agree that what the pastor does is his business, as long as I'm doing what I'm supposed to be doing. But I wouldn't be up in the church trying to lead somebody else if I was living foul, so I can't follow someone else who is. How can you follow someone you don't respect, and how can you respect a man with a wife on the front row, a girlfriend in the choir, and one on the usher board at the same time? That's just insane to me.

"Anyway, my friend and I got into a big argument over this and didn't call each other for three months. I thought about him everyday. But since he'd hung up on me, I felt he should make the first move to apologize. I was really hurt that he might let something like this come between us after all we'd been through. But then one day he beeped me, and when I called him back he was like, 'Hey Giovanni, how ya doing? Um, did you page me a while ago?' I paused—you know I had to savor the moment. Then I said, 'No, sweetie. I didn't page you, and you know it, so stop trying to play like you got a page from somebody you don't know. You'd know if I'd paged you 'cause I would have put in my number, so there would have been no doubt in your mind it was me. Where have you been?'

"We both cracked up laughing, happy that we'd been able to make fun of the situation. But since that time we don't discuss church too much. When we do, we keep it light so we don't offend each other.

"It's really nice to have someone to discuss my husband and children with who I know I can trust. If my husband pisses me off, I can call him and tell him what's going on, and he'll calm me down and get me to think about things before I jump to conclusions and make decisions that I'll later regret. I do the same thing for him. When he complains that his wife ain't giving him none, I ask him has he given her a reason to want to give him some. I've explained to him that women don't just turn their emotions off when they lay down like men do, and I think that has helped him to be more patient and understanding with her.

"One of the best things about our relationship is that I don't ever have to worry about him repeating anything I say to anyone else. Hell, both of us have too much to lose to be running off at the mouth. That's one of the things that has kept us together for so long. I often tell him that if I had it to do all over again, I'd find him and marry him. Then he could be my best friend, my lover, and my husband!"

Marcella, forty-something "As far as friends go, let me tell you a little story about what friends will do for you. About 15 years ago, there was a girl I used to call my best friend, until I found out she'd had sex with my husband in my driveway, in my car!" Marcella lit some incense and blew out the match.

"I guess I should have known 'cause she was always hanging around my house and was up in his face a lot more than she should have been anyway. Always grinning and smiling and shit when he came around—that should have been a clue right there, but I was so young and naive I never thought she'd do something like that. I was always taught not to get involved with another woman's boyfriend or husband, so I guess I thought everybody else was taught the same thing. Back on the islands, the whole community would look down on you for doing such a thing. But in this country, things are different.

"To make matters worse, about two weeks before I found out they'd had sex, this same girl had asked me to charge some furniture for her, and I did it, like a fool, because I felt sorry for her. She was a single woman with five little children, and the children were all sleeping in one queen-sized bed and using one dresser, so I thought I'd help her out.

"Well, one evening when I was getting my mail, my next door neighbor, a nosey old lady who was always at home watching everything that went on, stopped me and said, 'Sugar, I hate to tell you, but that little Tonya who you call your friend, ain't your friend at all. I been wanting to tel
but every time I saw you, I saw her too, so I couldn't get t
little slut been sliding across the street in that little tight, s
the past two weeks, coming over to your house late at night. Y

been meeting her out in the driveway, and they always get in the car, but the car don't never go nowhere. I reckon he figured you'd wake up if he started the motor, so they just sit out in the driveway and do their business at about 2:00 in the morning. Most of the time you can see him sittin' up in the seat, but you can't see her at all with her little nasty self. That's why she got all them damn babies by different men. She always been a ho, and her mama, God rest her soul, was the same way. It's just a damn shame.'

"I was floored. Here I thought he was up watching TV when he said he couldn't sleep, while instead he'd been screwing my friend. I was fit to be tied.

"I went over to her house and confronted her and she laughed, looked me straight in the eyes and said, 'Marcella, girl, I know you don't believe that crazy old lady. That old bitch ain't got nothing better to do than make up shit on me just because she never liked my mother and she's never liked me.'

"But the look on her face told me she was lying, and I told her I was going to kick her narrow, natural ass if I found out it was really true. She rushed me off, saying she had to go and would be over later to straighten it all out, but she never came over that evening, which was on a Thursday, and when I got home from work on Friday, she had moved out of that house with her kids and the furniture I'd bought. She just moved with all this shit I'd charged without saying a word.

"She wasn't working at the time and she'd been talking about moving in with some family down in Austin, Texas, so I figured that's where she'd gone. But what was I going to do—get the police to find her and make her bring my shit back? And my marriage was already on its way to being over anyway, so I knew that sorry husband of mine wouldn't confess, so there was no point in asking him.

"Well, guess what? About six months ago, I had to call the worker's compensation commission, and guess who I ended up talking to? Oh, she didn't know it was me, but I always take the name of the person helping me so I asked for her name. When she said 'Tonya,' I almost passed out. I asked her if she'd ever lived in the Dallas/Fort Worth metroplex area and she told me yes, trying to sound all proper and shit with her little country ass.

"Well, I let her finish giving me all the information I needed, then I asked her if she remembered a girl named Marcella who she used to be friends with, and after she beat around the bush for a minute, she told me that my accent sounded familiar. I told her who I was, and I know she almost dropped the phone. She started talking all fast and shit, asking me how I'd been, and lying about how happy she was to hear my voice. I just sat there and didn't say nothing because there was nothing to say. After she finished fumbling over her own words, the bitch had the nerve to invite me to come and see her if I was ever in Austin.

"As proper as I could, I told her ass off. I told her if I ever saw her black ass again, I was going to get a stick and beat the shit out of her for screwing my sorry-ass husband while her little crumb snatchers were sleeping on beds that I'd bought. I told her if I never see her bald-headed, no-man-having, green contact-wearing, ho ass again, that would be too soon and she'd better never come up this way to visit anybody and run into me because if she did, she'd regret the very day she met me. Then I just hung up the phone.

"Now I'm satisfied because even though she was known for having a quick tongue, for once in her sorry life, she didn't get a chance to say anything.

"To this day, the closest I get to friends is a close acquaintance. But I'll never have a best friend again."

Kiana, forty-something "When I was 21, there was a girl who was about 19 who was engaged to my brother, and we'd gotten as close as sisters. In fact, I treated her better than I treated my sister. She had a daughter who was around the same age as my daughter, and we were both single parents, so we decided to move in together to share expenses.

"We had a small apartment. Our rooms were kind of divided by a wall, but mine was on the far side and in order to get to the kitchen I had to go through her room. Well, I was walking through there to get ready for work one morning wearing nothing but my bra and panties, and there she was straddling some nigga', riding him for all he was worth. I was trying not to look because at first I figured it must be my brother, right? But when I came back through to go back to my room, she was sitting up in the bed, looking all stupid, and the guy in her bed was not my brother.

"I just kept on walking, finished getting dressed, and went on to work. It really made me mad because I felt like, number one, she disrespected me, and number two, if she was gonna fool around while messing with my brother, she could have at least waited until I was at work.

"So, when I got to work I called her and told her we needed to talk. That evening, after we'd discussed it, I packed my stuff and moved out because I didn't want to be in the middle of no mess like that. I liked her, but I loved my brother and I couldn't keep nothing like that from him. So I moved back home, and of course, I had to tell my brother what had happened.

"When I was talking to her, she acted like she didn't understand why I was so upset. She thought we were so close that she could trust me with something like that, but like I told her, blood is thicker than water. You don't take advantage of my friendship just because your ass got hot in the middle of the night.

"She said they would have gone to a motel, but she really didn't think he would still be there when I woke up, so she just let him spend the night. How dumb. I mean we were tight, really tight, and I was hurt. I couldn't even talk to her for a while after that first happened.

"After I finally calmed down, I called her and told her it wasn't the fact that she was messing around on my brother that hurt me so much because people do stuff like that all the time. It was the fact that she didn't respect me. She didn't care how I'd feel about seeing her in that position, and by doing that she walked all over me and him, like she really didn't care about either one of us.

"She asked me to please forgive her, but I was never able to and I'll never forget that. My brother was heartbroken, and I've always resented her for that. So, I don't have too many women friends, you know? You just can't trust them."

Veronica, thirty-something

"Now you know I have a lot of acquaintances," Veronica began. "But I can honestly say I'd much rather have male rather than female friends. Why? Hell, that's easy to explain.

"I met this girl when I was going to college and we became best friends. We used to hang out together with our boyfriends and do just about everything together, right? Well, we both ended up marrying the guys we were dating, so we went from becoming best friends to being very close as young married couples, and we used to get together all the time. We'd go clubbing together on Saturday nights, go to church and then bar-b-que at the park on Sundays, and even take turns planning double dates.

"After we'd been married about two years, my husband and I ended up moving to another state because of our jobs and my friend and her husband divorced. We felt kinda bad that their marriage hadn't worked out, but then both of them remarried about a year later and everything was cool. Since her ex-husband's new wife wanted him to cut all ties with his former wife's friends, we lost contact with him. But I remained close to her for the next two years or so, speaking by phone, writing letters, and sending cards because we were both so busy. Then she finally decided to come for a visit without her husband, and that's when I realized why her first husband had divorced her.

"This child had lost her real mind. I knew she'd been saved and was calling herself an evangelist, and I had no problem with that. But I also knew something was wrong with her calling her senior pastor every morning while she was at my house, long distance. I'd try to give her some privacy when she was on the phone, but the calls lasted so long that I just couldn't stay in my room and wait for her to clear the line. Hell, she was in my damn house. Why was I tip-toeing around like I didn't want to offend her? And the way she was whispering and giggling, there ain't no way in hell they could have been talking about God, okay? It was very obvious that the two of them had been touching and agreeing, but not on nothing in the Bible, and she was acting as if I was blind, deaf, and dumb.

"Well, she'd planned to stay with us for two weeks, which was too damn long for me in the first place, but after that first five days, I'd had enough of her getting up and going through my refrigerator and fixing breakfast for me and my husband without so much as asking me if I minded. So, I decided I was gonna make up some lie that we planned to visit family in another town for the weekend to get her to leave, but she still didn't get the hint. At least she didn't act like she did.

"Just when I figured there was no other way out except to tell her that she had overstayed her visit, wore out her welcome, whatever the hell I needed to say to get her to pack up her shit and leave, she made it easy for me. I walked in on her late one night while she was on the phone, and she didn't even know I was standing there.

" 'Hey, boo,' she said in a voice so sweet it sounded like somebody else. 'Yeah, I miss you too. I been playing with myself every night thinking about you, but I can't come home yet 'cause he might not think I'm serious about leaving him if I come back too soon . . . . Yeah, it's nice out here, but my friend is a trip. I told her I call you every day so we can pray together and she's so dumb, she believes it. She living in this nice house and all, telling me her husband is so good to her, but I'll bet if she left me here with him for about 45 minutes, and I gave him some of this poonany, he'd tell her to pack her shit and leave. You know how I do it.' Then she laughed a deep, what she apparently thought was a sexy laugh, while still trying to be quiet, but it was too late.

"I turned the lights on her crazy ass and said, 'Bitch, if you don't get your hands out of your little funky crotch and get off my damn phone right now, you gonna be speaking in tongues, wishing your pastor could come save you while my foot is in your ass. How dare you come into my house and take my kindness for granted, when you don't even deserve it. You got ten minutes to get your little raggedy shit that you brought in that little raggedy-ass suitcase you had to borrow from somebody, and get out of my house. Ten minutes, you hear me? And don't say shit because if you do, I'm calling your husband to tell him what's really going on. In the meantime I'm going to get my gun, just in case you think I'm playing games with your stupid ass. Now you and your pastor pray about that.'

"Honey, her eyes got all big and she hurried up and got her stuff together while I stood at the door and watched her. I didn't even give her time to change clothes or call a cab or nothing. I just pushed her ass out the front door and slammed it right in her face. How's that for a friend?"

AFFAIRS

af-fair (a-far) noun

A private matter; personal concern.

A matter causing scandal and controversy.

A love affair; liaison.

It's not a good feeling when you find out you're being cheated on, but oh, how well we can rationalize it away when we're the ones doing the cheating. All of us, I suspect, have heard about somebody being cheated on, and all of us most likely know somebody who's cheated. People have been having affairs for hundreds of years and will continue to have them, regardless of the right or wrong of it. If you were to ask me, I'd say the main reason we're told that affairs are wrong, beyond the religious reason, is because an affair causes your relationship to lose its innocence. It won't take you long to realize that if you can have an affair and still go on about the day-to-day business of living with him, acting like nothing is happening on the side, what's to stop him from doing the same thing? From the time you have your first affair, no matter if your mate is actually going where he says he's going or doing what he says he's doing, you'll always have this little seed of doubt, and you know why? Because you've lost the innocence. You become very much aware of what could be going on because you've done it yourself. Those blinders that you've worn into that relationship are irrevocably taken away, and there is no way you can get them back, so your perception of things, real or imagined, become almost too painfully clear.

"Love does not begin and end the way we seem to think it does.
Love is a battle; love is a war; love is a growing up."
—*Unknown*

"That's what adultery is, a meanness, and a stealing, a taking away from someone what should be theirs, a great selfishness, and surrounded and guarded by lies lest it should be found out. And out of this meanness and this selfishness and this lying flow love and joy and peace, beyond anything that can be imagined."
—*Rose Macaulay, 1956*

"Bigamy is having one husband too many. Monogamy is the same."
—*Anonymous woman in Erica Jong, Fear of Flying, 1972*

"The compulsion to find a lover and a husband in a single person has doomed more women to misery than any other illusion."
—*Carolyn Helbrun, 1988*

"Never tell a loved one of an infidelity; you would be badly rewarded for your trouble. Although one dislikes being deceived, one likes even less to be undeceived."
—*Ninon de Cencios, 1665*

"Show me a woman who doesn't feel guilty, and I'll show you a man."
—*Erica Jong, 1973*

Giovanni, forty-something "You know what I think?" Giovanni pulled off her gold hoop earrings and laid them on the table next to her. "I think people have affairs because they get plain old bored. If you get married before you're 25 or 30, you don't really know what those vows mean. I know I didn't. It was years before I realized what 'in sickness and health, til death do us part' meant. It means that you stay together no matter what. You stay together if he doesn't have a job, if he's broke, if he's sorry, lazy, not the perfect lover, or not a good provider." She rubbed her earlobes. " 'In sickness and health til death do us part' means that regardless of the circumstances, you're supposed to be true to your spouse."

Porsche, forty-something "Women are romantic, emotional creatures and tend to have affairs for far different reasons than men," Porsche said. She'd and I were both silent as we watched the ducks lazily circling the pond from our place on the blanket. She inhaled deeply and closed her eyes to relax. She'd stated earlier that she knew her husband was going to pick a fight about something when she got home. It never failed. He'd bought her a birthday cake one time and some sleazy outfit that she'd never think of wearing and when she didn't show the proper appreciation for it, he picked up the cake and threw it at her. She'd been physically put out of the house by him on more than one occasion and belittled more times than she could even remember. She'd married him right out of college, but it had been the biggest mistake of her life, and she paid for it every waking moment.

"Your lover will tell you things your husband doesn't. Things like, 'You have beautiful teeth, sexy legs, you smell so good, you look so pretty.' I like to be complimented. I like to feel special. I like excitement, so the affair becomes thrilling because it's something forbidden, something new and different. My affair has made me feel like a teenager all over again. It's been so long since I had butterflies in my stomach, that I'd forgotten such a feeling existed."

Porsche set her drink down and pulled her knees to her chest, curling her arms around them and resting her chin there. "I think a man has an affair because he enjoys the feel of a different woman, he enjoys the sex. He might not be getting any at home or if he's getting some, it's not as often or as freaky as he likes. The other woman might make him feel like the world revolves around him, the same way his wife used to make him feel before the kids, bills, and problems with the in-laws came along."

Giovanni, forty-something "When I had an affair, I was at a point in my life where I wasn't satisfied with marriage or myself. When he asked me to come over to his house I warned him up front that I didn't have the most fabulous body in the world. I was self-conscious about my body, and no other man had seen it since I'd been married, and that had been ten years. Well, why did he say, 'I'm into women, not little girls?' What did he tell me that for? Cause when he said that, I got to thinking . . . ooooooh . . . I'm a woman." Giovanni rolled her eyes towards the ceiling and made herself even more comfortable on the sofa as she clicked her tongue. "Like I didn't know that already." She ran her long elegant fingers through her new hairstyle. That day her hair was light brown with honey-blonde highlights. Giovanni was known to change hairstyles frequently.

"He completely turned me on. I would've been happy just to sit down somewhere and stare up in his face all day and probably would've left my husband for him if he would've treated me halfway decent.

"His body was like black silk—skin so smooth that the thought of it gives me chills. And his ass? Two words describe it—taut and fine. I hadn't seen an ass like that before, and I haven't seen one like it since. He had these big, muscular thighs and a stomach that looked like he spent an hour a day doing sit-ups. And I'm not even going to talk about his arms and shoulders, but I will tell you this: He could make me wet just by licking his lips. He was 6 feet 2 inches, 180 pounds, bowlegged, and had the sexiest mouth I'd ever seen. We slept together a week after we met." She pushed some books off of the table that were marked for clearance, propped her feet up and sneaked a peek at me to see if she'd been able to shock me with her honesty. The only thing I was shocked about was how nicely her hair fell back into place each and every time she plowed her fingers through it.

"He invited me over to his house for a drink one evening. An hour after I'd arrived, I was sitting in this plush armchair that was wide enough to seat two people and was sipping on this marvelous strawberry daiquiri he'd made with fresh strawberries and Jamaican rum. He turned the lights down, took off his shirt, sat down on the floor between my knees and handed me some massage oil and asked me to massage his neck and shoulders because he was kind of sore from an earlier workout. I was only too glad to oblige because I'd been waiting for a legitimate reason to get my hands on him since the first time I'd seen him. I knew I was in trouble when he took that shirt off, and I got a close up of his chest and stomach. There wasn't an extra ounce of fat anywhere. His chest was wide and the muscles firm, and his stomach muscles just rippled when he moved. He looked just like one of those underwear models, but ten times sexier.

"I hadn't gone over to his house with the intention of having sex with him, but I must've been expecting something, or why else would I be wearing my sexiest underwear?

"After I'd massaged his shoulders for a while, with both of us pretending to watch TV, and I couldn't tell you if you offered me a million dollars what it was we watched, he got up and walked around the chair to stand behind me. He started to caress my neck, arms, and breasts, and by the time he leaned down and bit me on my neck and started to suck on my earlobe I lost all sense of time and myself. I managed to stand up, and we kissed all the way to his bedroom.

"When he lay me on the bed and began to undress me, he took the time to fold every piece of my clothing then got on his knees, pulled me to the edge of the mattress, and began to give me the best oral sex I'd had in my life—and not one time did I think about my body not fitting a perfect image. I was too much into how he was making me feel to even begin worrying about stuff like that."

Giovanni reached for a paperback book similar to the ones that she had placed on the floor, noticed that the sale price wasn't marked and put it in a different stack.

"He said, 'Talk to me.Tell me what you want.' Now I wasn't much of a talker, but before we got done, I must've talked and hollered up a storm.

When we finished, he left the bed to go clean himself up and that's when all hell broke loose.

" 'Damn!' I heard him say. I got up and grabbed his robe that he'd left at the foot of the bed for me and ran into the bathroom to find out what was wrong.

" 'Look what you did!' He was staring at himself in the mirror and pointing at the large purplish hickey on the side on his neck.

"Now, since I hadn't read the manual on the dos and don'ts of having the perfect affair, it was obvious that I'd made a pretty big mistake. Since then I've determined that the ten big DON'TS are as follows:

1. *Don't bite or suck too hard.*
2. *Don't scratch.*
3. *Don't wear perfume.*
4. *Don't wear lipstick.*
5. *Don't plan on doing it in the bed after the first time because that's where I do it with my wife/girlfriend, and I do have some morals.*
6. *Don't plan on using the good towels and if you insist on washing up afterwards or if you must take a shower, please make it quick.*
7. *Don't plan on staying around too long after we're through screwing because my wife or girlfriend might come home unexpectedly.*
8. *Don't expect me to call you tomorrow—or maybe not even the next few days—unless I feel the urge to get with you again.*
9. *Don't expect me to take you out to lunch or dinner or be seen in any public place with you, whatsoever.*
10. *Don't fall in love with me because you will definitely be hurt when you find out that I have no intention of letting myself feel the same way.*

"Simply stated, I was way out of my league, totally confused and humiliated. I never had to worry about holding back when having sex, and hadn't he just told me to talk to him and tell him what I wanted? What I wanted was to be able to have sex without having to worry about remembering not to suck on his neck or grip his shoulders too hard. After all, he was a single man. I had more to lose than he did, so why was he the one with all the damn rules?

"It went on that way between the two of us for a whole year. We'd have this wild, crazy intense sex, but after each encounter, he'd act shitty until he wanted to have sex again. And I was so infatuated with him that I went along with it." Giovanni got up and started to rearrange books on the shelf directly in front of us.

Talking over her shoulder she continued: "He actually said to me one time, 'I like you and I really want to be with you, but I constantly have to remind myself that you're a married woman and I can't have you. I can't just let myself go because when it's over it's got to be over. I can't let myself fall in love with you.' But still, like a fool, I allowed myself to fall in love with him."

A bitter laugh escaped her lips. "I can't say the experience was wasted because I learned a good, hard lesson. I learned that an affair is just an affair. There has to be an end to it. Don't think about getting your heart involved; that way you can't get hurt. Don't think it's going to amount to something one day because it won't. Even if we ended up with one another, I wouldn't trust him and he wouldn't trust me, so why bother?"

Vanessa, thirty-something "There's no way you can be in love with two men at the same time, at least not equally. You might tell both of them you love them, and you might even believe it yourself, but somebody is being shortchanged. I know because I've done it."

Miss Charsie, fifty-something "If my husband had an affair I just couldn't stay with him because I could never forgive him for cheating on me. When I trust somebody, I trust them with all my heart and soul, and when they take that trust away, nothing's left." Miss Charsie was adamant in her response.

I played the devil's advocate and asked, "Would you be willing to give up the person you love knowing you might not ever have him in your life again just because he made a mistake?"

"Having sex outside of your marriage is not a mistake, and I know for a fact that I could not stay with a man who betrayed me. There is no excuse he could offer me that would make it all right. To me it would be just as bad as child molestation. There's no excuse and no explanation for it."

"But think about it," I insisted. I was pressing like this because the shit had happened to a close girlfriend of mine, and she hadn't left her husband. She'd told me that it had happened after they'd been married a year, she'd been young and innocent, and not too crazy about sex but doing the best she knew how. She and her husband had been at a Christmas party at someone's house when she noticed that he had disappeared a little too long. When she found him in one of the host's back bedrooms, she was confronted with the sight of him on his knees with his tongue between the thighs of a strange woman, but it was clear that the woman wasn't a stranger to him the way she was calling him by his nickname and grinding her crotch in his face.

So, I continued to pressure Miss Charsie, wondering what it was that made some women stay when they found out that their man had cheated and why some women left.

"But Miss Charsie, look at it this way. This is a man you love and he made a mistake that didn't have anything to do with how he felt about you. It was just meaningless sex, and you're telling me that you'd be willing to give up that man and your lifestyle for that one indiscretion?"

She did her best to explain it to me. "First of all, sex isn't meaningless. If he took the time to have sex with her, then it meant something. It would mean a hell of a lot to me to find out that my man has been intimate with another woman, to find out that he has given her something that should belong to me only. I'm sorry, but he'd have to go because I couldn't be with him anymore. I couldn't be with him and live a life all the time wondering whether everything he says to me is a lie. When I love someone, I love with everything that I have. I can't do it halfway. If he cheats on me, he's hurt me and when he hurts me there's no going back. I just can't be with a person who would do something like that. I don't care how much I love him."

I kept on pushing. "So, no second chances?"

"No second chances."

Sadie, fifty-something "I think people have affairs because they want something different. A married woman might not feel like having sex because she's tired. She'll get home from work, probably have to fuss at her kids about one thing or the other, cook dinner, clean up the kitchen, and probably wash a load of clothes. By the time it's all said and done it's bedtime and the last thing she's gonna have on her mind is trying to find some sexy negligee to prance around in before lying down," Sadie shrugged. "I'm sorry but it just ain't gonna' happen. The only thing that woman's thinking about is putting on a T-shirt, some comfortable cotton underwear, brushing her teeth, getting in the bed, and going to sleep." She held her hand up like she was stopping traffic. "Don't come up to me trying to be Don Juan when all I'm thinking about is lying my tired ass down and getting some rest."

Ruby, forty-something "Have I ever had an affair?" Ruby repeated the question I'd just put to her. "A few years ago, if you would've asked me that question I would've laughed and said, 'Affair? Me? Oh hell no, that's the worse thing in the world you can do to somebody you love.' I knew how much it could hurt 'cause it had happened to me. There was never any doubt in my mind that I would even think of being unfaithful to my husband. I didn't daydream about other men, didn't even wish for another man. I was more shocked than anyone else would've been, had they known, when I found myself in an affair that lasted for more than five years. The experience was both good and bad, and notice I use the past tense because no matter what anybody tells you, eventually the affair ends.

"The first time we spoke to one another was on the elevator of the building where my dance studio is located. I had just left the studio, and he'd just gotten off work too. When I got outside I noticed that it had started to rain—just a light sprinkle. Well, he was right beside me as we stepped outside, so he offered me his umbrella. He is very much a gentleman. Now every time it sprinkles, I think about him. Anyway, we introduced ourselves and both went on about our business of getting home.

"After that first hello I found myself looking for him in the parking lot or getting on or off the elevator. He located my office number from the building directory and started calling. At first it was just every now and then, but it wasn't long before it was every day. I was halfway teasing when I warned him he'd spoil me if he kept it up, and I didn't know how much I looked forward to hearing from him until he didn't call for a couple of days. At that time, I was too naive to realize that I'd already fallen in love with him—or at least the idea of him.

"We met in March, talked off and on until June, then he invited me over to his house." Ruby sighed deeply as she reminisced. "We were sitting on his sofa one minute and kissing the next. It was like time slowed to a crawl because I can remember every single thing about that day down to what we were both wearing. He came towards me from his kitchen, carrying two glasses of ice tea because I'd told him I was thirsty. He was smiling. When I asked him about the smile he simply said, 'I can't believe you came.' Well I couldn't believe it either, but I'm sure he knew that.

"He sat down next to me, put the glasses on the table in front of us, then leaned over and touched his lips to mine. It was nice and gentle at first, like he didn't want to scare me off. But it wasn't long before we'd forgotten all about being gentle. I hadn't kissed like that in forever. The whole time we kissed I was telling myself, 'You can handle this. It's nothing—just an experiment.' It was a fantasy kiss, you know, those kisses that melt your insides and you get so wet you have to change your underwear? That's the kind of kiss it was. Each and every time we talked on the phone my panties got wet, and we could just be talking about something as simple as the weather, but the timbre of his voice just worked for me.

"I came from his first kiss, and the only thing that kept me from sleeping with him that day was the fact that his phone started ringing. That's what brought me to my senses. It was like an alarm. If it hadn't been for that interruption, I would've been laying right there on his couch, making love with him.

"By the time the phone stopped ringing, I'd gotten the chance to pull myself together. I was nervous, confused, and embarrassed when I mumbled, 'I believe I'd better go.' He was a gentleman about it because he didn't try to stop me. I think he realized that this was something that I'd never done before, but I was obviously on his mind as much as he was on mine. When he called me to come back over after only a few days had passed, I went and by then we both knew what was going to happen."

Ruby fiddled with her two-carat diamond wedding ring. "Before the front door closed, we were all over each other. My purse went in one direction and my shoes in another. The sex was good and from that time on, no matter when or where he wanted to make love, and no matter when or where I wanted to make love, we were always ready for each other and every time was like the first time.

"He was divorced, but he did have a serious girlfriend. What were the rules for that? What could a married woman ask of a single man? Was I supposed to give him an ultimatum and say 'I don't want you to have a girlfriend because just the thought of you with another woman makes me crazy'? I didn't have the right to tell him that, and we never even mentioned her name. When we talked about our significant others, which was as little as possible, we just used she or he to describe them. It was like even letting their names enter into our conversation would interfere with our fantasy of one another. We were extremely compatible, but it just wasn't the right time in life for us, and he realized that from the start, but I didn't want to. I kept trying to make the relationship into something it could never be. I think I loved him as much as I'd ever loved anyone in my life, but my mistake was that I didn't try to hide it.

"I have to give it to him, though," Ruby said smiling. "He never tried to jeopardize my marriage. He never told me he loved me, but I like to believe that he did. We were still lovers when he got engaged and married his girlfriend. You can't even begin to imagine how much that hurt. You don't know how hard it is to have the man you love tell you that he has asked another woman to marry him. It's not like I didn't expect it to happen some day. I just didn't want to believe it could. But whenever he started off a sentence with 'Well, guess what?' I always knew it would be something that I wouldn't like and he'd never have to finish because I would always guess. I didn't want to picture him proposing to her over a candlelight dinner with soft music in the background or the smile on her face when he put the ring on her finger, but I imagined it anyway, and that time when he said, 'Guess what?' I was devastated.

"Then no more than two years after I went through the experience of him getting married, and yes, we were still seeing each other, he again said, 'Well, guess what?'

" 'She's pregnant right?' I responded, dreading confirmation. But as usual, I hit the nail right on the head. And so it went. Not a very pleasant period in my life, let me tell you, but I suffered through it because I loved him.

"If I would've known how much hurt would be in store for me, I wouldn't have given my heart so freely, and even though I knew what I was doing wasn't right, the feelings I had for him were totally honest, and

I never felt guilty about being with him because I loved him. I never got that 'it's not supposed to be this good with someone else' feeling. When I was with him I felt like it was just meant to be. He was who I was supposed to be with.

"The last time he asked me that horrible 'Well, guess what?' question I couldn't even begin to guess because I thought, what else could there be? How much worse could it get? He'd gotten married, had a baby, bought a new house, found a wonderful job. I couldn't imagine, but I knew whatever it was didn't bode well for me. I took a deep breath and responded, 'What?' 'I'm moving to the west coast in three months. I got a promotion.'" Ruby sighed like she was tired, but pressed on like she was glad to be able to go ahead and talk about it and get if off of her chest once and for all.

"Well, that time my heart broke for good because he definitely had a choice as to whether he wanted to go or stay and he chose to go, and I had a hard time dealing with that. How could you have an affair with somebody for five years and then just up and say, 'Guess what? I'm moving.' There was no, 'I'm thinking about moving' or 'there's a possibility that I might be moving.' When he told me about it, the decision was already made. He didn't ask for any input from me. His bags were nearly packed. When it came down to it, I finally realized that I had no say. I was merely the woman who had been making love with him for the last five years, nothing more and nothing less." Ruby sat up straighter and there was a knowing glint in her eye that I was sure hadn't been there before she'd set out on this topic. Looking at her, I knew for certain she wouldn't enter into a relationship like that again without having her guard up.

"To this day I still don't understand it. I don't understand how someone you've shared the most secret parts of yourself with can just out of the blue and over the phone say 'I'm moving.' Come to think of it, anytime he had news like that to give me it was over the phone. When he dropped the news that he was leaving I felt like he was simply saying, 'The sex was good. I enjoyed the conversations, but that's all there was to it.'

"He never told me anything like 'Hey, I really hate the fact that it's got to be this way. I'm sad that I'm leaving you, but it's really for the best.' All he said was he was leaving, and all I did was cry.

"He said, 'We'll still talk. We'll keep in touch.' We went from talking almost every day to maybe once every month or so, and I'm doing good if I hear from him that often. He's even come back home a few times and hasn't contacted me. I guess some people have to be knocked over the head a few times before they get it. I still can't believe how he took what I felt for him so lightly. It was like my love for him didn't mean a thing. I can't even begin to explain how much he hurt me and I still get angry when I allow myself to think about it because I still have strong feelings for him." Ruby looked at me and held up her right hand like she was swearing in a court of law. "I know one thing for sure. I won't be going through that kind of shit again."

Bianca, thirty-something "My sister had a baby for a man who was engaged to be married to someone else." Bianca motioned to the bartender for another drink. "I think she was hoping he'd break off the engagement and marry her instead, but that didn't happen. He married his fiancee of two years and failed to break the news to her that another woman was carrying his child, hoping and praying she'd never find out.

"My sister was given a baby shower on the day of his wedding and after all the gifts were opened, she said to nobody in particular, 'Well, they should be married by now.' She was trying to laugh and joke about it, but I could tell she wasn't laughing inside.

"His wife must've heard rumors about the baby because she called my sister right after she'd given birth and started asking questions. Her husband had told her they were just good friends, and he helped her off and on since the baby's father was nowhere to be found. Can you believe it? This married man was giving my sister money, bought her a car, and still had the nerve to try to pass it off like he was this good guy doing a close friend a favor.

"I don't understand how his wife didn't realize what was happening. He even wrote my sister checks from a joint account that he and his wife shared." Bianca clicked her tongue and reached for her drink. "Baby, that couldn't have been me. I would've acted like such a fool he would've been scared to sleep at night. I'm glad my sister didn't marry him because if he'd do that to his wife, he'd do it to her. She's better off without him."

Kat, thirty-something "Let me tell you something, baby," Kat dug in her purse for a cigarette. I swear, she only smoked because it brought attention to those sexy lips of hers. She lit the cigarette, inhaled and sighed like it was the best thing she'd tasted all day. "Damn, I know I need to give this shit up, but I can't. I have so few pleasures in my life as it is." She took another deep puff, then put the cigarette out. "I don't ever smoke the whole thing and I know I'm wasting a lot of money, but what's money when you're doing something you like?" She kicked off one of her high-heeled sandals and started massaging toes that were painted tangerine orange.

"So, you want to know what I think about infidelity?" I nodded and glanced longingly at the cigarette that was still smoldering in the electric blue ceramic ashtray. I hadn't smoked a cigarette in years, but I still craved one every now and then.

"Well, for one thing, I don't think affairs are always about sex. My husband has a high sex drive. The man would make love to me every night if I'd let him, but he doesn't have a romantic bone in his body. He's forgotten about all the sweet things that are needed to keep a relationship going. He's forgotten about the flowers, the wining and dining, the dancing. So, I for one know why I'm having an affair. I'm not going to lie. I'm doing it for the sweet things. I'm doing it for the romance, for the flowers I know he's going to show up with, and for those times when he sees me undressed, stops dead in his tracks, and says 'Daaammnnn!'

"My lover knows a woman's body the way Mozart knew how to compose. He reads everything he can get his hands on about male and female relationships. He doesn't take it for granted that just because he has a penis and I have a vagina all he needs to do to make me feel good is put it in. He knows more about the female anatomy than a gynecologist. Whew." Kat blew out some air and fanned her face. "I know it's not just these jeans I'm wearing that's making me hot." When I asked her if he could kiss, Kat shook her head and lowered her eyes. "I can't even begin to tell you how good he kisses. He has these deep, sexy, wet, delicious kisses. You know that little piece of flesh that holds your tongue to the bottom of your mouth? It's sore for at least two days afterwards, and I think about him every time I raise my tongue to lick my lips.

"I figure I can't ever take back what I give him, and when I told him that he said, 'I can't take mine back either.' That's when I told him that his could be flushed down the toilet.

"It's true. Think about it. And he knows I have certain rules. For instance, if he wants to see me and make love to me, then he needs to buy the dinner and he needs to pay for the hotel. I should be worth at least that much to him.

"He wanted to take me to Jamaica, but he suggested that I buy my own ticket so no one, meaning his wife, would get suspicious. Well, needless to say, we're not going to Jamaica." She kicked off her other sandal and began to massage that foot. "If a man wants to take me on vacation, all I should have to show up with is my purse. I shouldn't even have to carry a change of underwear if I don't want to. I want it to be like this . . . ." She pantomimed taking out a wallet and handing it over . . . . 'Here baby, if you want something, get it.'

"When he tried that thing about me getting my own ticket, I told him that for all the reading he did about relationships, he still didn't know how to carry off a rendezvous. He laughed, but you know what? He wanted to see just how far he could go with me, and if I would've bought that ticket, it would've been fine with him.

"The orgasms I have with my husband are nothing like the ones I have with my lover. I enjoy everything we do when we make love. I asked him once if the vagina felt different from woman to woman. He said that all a man feels is a soft, warm place. The only difference is in the shape of the woman's body and how you feel about her. He said that when it gets down to the sex, it all feels the same. I'd always thought that just like every man was different in size, thickness, and length, every woman was different."

Porsche, forty-something

When Porsche began to talk about her lover, her whole face lit up.

"My affair began over a business lunch. My lover, who is a physician like I am, was thinking about consolidating his practice with three or four other successful physicians and wanted to know if I was interested. We'd known each other for a few years and had run into one another at various social and professional functions over the years. While I wasn't willing to consolidate my practice, I did have to tell him something that had been on my mind for quite some time, so when I couldn't take it any longer, I put my fork down and said, 'I need to tell you something and I hope I don't embarrass you.' He asked what it was and kept on about the business of eating. I guess he thought the business portion of the meal was over because I'd said no to the consolidation for the fourth time.

"I said, 'I am very attracted to you.' I'll never forget the expression on his face when I said that. He looked halfway shocked and totally serious because he immediately laid his fork down, and replied, 'Well, what the hell are we going to do about it?'

"I was stunned when he asked me that because I'd expected him to respond, 'Well thank you, that's very nice.' I wasn't prepared for a 'Well, what the hell are we going to do about it?' I got real nervous and stammered out, 'We're not going to do anything about it. I just wanted to tell you how I felt.' " Porsche began to twist a braid around one finger, as was her habit as she stared unseeingly at the others in the park. "Now remember, this was coming from a woman who had never even thought about being with someone outside of her marriage.

"He said, 'So you tell me you're attracted to me, make me lose my appetite when I got all this food on my plate, then go on to tell me you don't want to do anything about it?' I was almost tongue-tied by then, but I seriously hadn't expected him to respond that way. We tried to finish eating lunch but ended up only moving the food around on our plates, so we gave up and trudged back to his car for the ride back to my office. After he'd parked the car in front of my building, he turned and asked me for a hug. He said, 'I just want to feel you, I want to see what you feel like.' I nodded, but I was stiff and nervous. He gave me this tender hug, and it really turned me on.

"After that we started to talk on the phone about once every other week. I'd call him or he'd call me. Then we both attended a big conference out of town.

"I'd bought all these sexy nighties and stuff, just in case, but I kept telling myself, 'I'm not going to do this. I'm not going to let anything happen. Well if anything happens, I'm not going to try to stop it, but I'm not going to initiate it.' Well, he was obviously thinking the same thing, but I didn't know it. We got there and the atmosphere was perfect for romance, but I just couldn't approach him that way. I'd never been outside my marriage before, and the idea of it scared me. Nine months had passed since I'd told him how I felt, and the fire that he had started inside of me with that one comment and that sweet hug was still there. And let me tell you, nine months is a long time to fantasize about being with someone.

"He came to my room one evening for a drink and was sitting in a chair talking to me. It was getting late, so I said, 'You've got to go. You can't be in my room.' I was getting weak and I was scared because I was still thinking at that point in time that if you have an affair and you're married, you'll have to go home, confess, and get a divorce.

"We went on a date the next night, and of course, we started talking about sex. Why is it that when you're attracted to someone the conversation always seems to turn to sex? He told me his wife withholds sex as a form of punishment when she's mad at him, and he told me all about the problems they were having. I told him my problems, too, because we all have them, but we still didn't have sex that night. We didn't make love at all the whole time we were there. We didn't sleep together until a few months later, and by then I couldn't use the excuse that it just happened. I'd had a long time to think about it. Later he told me, 'Yes, I did want to be with you, but I wasn't about to initiate it. I would've gone along with it, but there was no way I would ever initiate it.'

"Seven months later when we went out of town for another conference I finally got up the nerve to approach him. I told him that I wanted him to come to my room after dinner was over. It was hard to sit through that dinner and keep my mind on the speaker. All I could think about was the fact that I'd invited this married man up to my room. I was a married woman, and I hoped I wasn't making the biggest mistake of my life. Right after dinner, in which I could barely finish my salad let alone even touch the rest of the meal, I pleaded a headache and declined a friend's offer of getting a drink at the bar. Instead, I rushed up to my room to shower and change. About an hour later he knocked at my door, and I took a deep breath and went to let him in. He'd taken off his dress shirt and pants and had changed into a black turtleneck and khaki pants, and he was looking and smelling good. I had deliberated between wearing my robe with nothing underneath or my floor length nightie, but I opted for a simple linen dress with no underwear. I could only be so bold.

"I offered him a drink and he sat down in the chair across from my bed while I perched at the end of the bed, making sure to keep my legs crossed because I didn't want him to see everything all at once.

"When he asked me why I'd invited him to my room I told him that it was obvious that he wasn't prepared to make the first move and that it had been about a year since I'd told him I was attracted to him. That's when he told me that he didn't want to be the one to make the first move because it was obvious that I was wrestling with the rights and wrongs of having an affair, and that he didn't want to push me into doing something I wasn't too sure about. He explained that he had had one affair in the past, but that it had ended several years ago. We talked about that for a while. Then I poured him another drink and poured myself one and actually got up the nerve to go over to him and sit in his lap. When I did that I noticed that he wasn't as cool as he was pretending to be because he had an awesome erection. After I'd leaned in and kissed him he asked me if I was sure this was something I wanted to do, and when I told him yes, he took over from there. And let me tell you, it was well worth the wait—guilt and all.

"I'm so in love with him, but I hope he doesn't break my heart. And while we may never be together as a couple, I think we'll always be a part of each other's lives. I've tried to end it several times because I know it's not going anywhere. I'm one of those people who needs a goal. I've got to be moving towards something and this relationship seems endless. I told him when we first got together that our limit was five years and if nothing materialized in five years, I was going to end it because I didn't want to do this forever. Five years is a long time to figure out if you want to be together or not. My New Year's resolution this year was that I was going to stop seeing him, and I meant that until I saw him two days later. He came all prepared to break up because I'd told him that was what I wanted. He said, 'This will kill me, but if being your friend means I can still talk to you or we can go to lunch every now and then, I'm fine.'

"It's been ten years and many New Year's resolutions later, and we're still lovers."

Cheyanne, forty-something Cheyanne, was just about finished talking with me when I asked her about her affairs with married men. "I dated this one married man for three years, but it ended after we came back from a four-day weekend in Lake Tahoe." She adjusted the drape around my shoulders and picked up her can of Diet Coke. She drank Diet Coke like other people drink coffee.

"Of course he went and explained his absence to his wife in a way I'd clearly warned him not to. He has a grown son from a previous marriage, and he told his wife that the two of them were going to go on a fishing trip. I told him that wasn't a good idea because she could always check that out, but he ignored my advice, shrugged his shoulders, and said, 'She ain't gonna call me.' Sure enough, the wife called the son's job, telling whoever answered the phone that she was the son's girlfriend and when he came to the phone she hung up. By the time my lover got home, every lock on every door had been changed. He was calling me no more than an hour after he'd dropped me off saying, 'She knows,' and I asked, 'Knows what?'

" 'She knows about us.' I guess she'd agreed to let him in the house once he confessed to his wrongdoing, and he called me to break things off.

"I said, 'Who is this?' The whole time I was thinking fast and good thing too, because she was on the other line.

" 'I'm telling you, she knows,' he said again, slowly this time, like I didn't understand English or something.

"I continued to play it cool and replied, 'You must have the wrong number.' Well I guess she'd heard all she could stand, but I wasn't confessing to nothing. If he was caught, then that was between him and his wife. She didn't find out about it from me because I am not the kind of woman to be calling another woman's house, hanging up, and shit.

" 'You know who this is, bitch!' she screamed into the phone. 'You were with my husband all weekend.'

"I said, 'Look, I don't know who or what you're talking about and I told you you've got the wrong number,' and I hung up. I didn't feel bad about it because I'd plainly told him not to use his son as an alibi. I found out later that she'd become suspicious because he'd called me one time while the two of them were on vacation. I guess she found the number on the hotel bill and wrote it down. When he went on vacation with me, she called my shop, found out I was on vacation and put two and two together.

"We broke up after that, and I eventually started seeing someone else. This new guy was divorced and crazy about me. At least he acted like it because he cooked dinner for me, washed and ironed my clothes, and everything. He was too nice, as a matter of fact, and I didn't know how to appreciate it because I started seeing somebody else at the same time. This other man lived around the corner from me, and when my boyfriend was at work I'd invite him over. It was my house, after all, and he was a damn good lover. Well, I invited him over one time too many because we'd just gotten naked when the front door opened and there stood my boyfriend. I was so scared that I started to laugh hysterically. I didn't know what else to do.

"My boyfriend finally said, 'Look, man, I don't want to fight you, just pick up your clothes and leave.' After he left, my boyfriend turned to me and said, 'If you think you need to screw around, I'd appreciate it if you didn't do it in this house.' He didn't hit me, curse me out or anything. So, I said okay and the next time I met the other man at a hotel." Cheyanne stopped talking when she heard me gasp in disbelief. "I've already told you I'm not used to a man who treats me too nice. Frankly, I was surprised that the other man was still bold enough to want to see me after that little episode, but when sex is involved, what do you expect?

"One time I'd no sooner pulled into the parking lot of the hotel before a car came speeding past, almost running into me. Well, of course it was my boyfriend. He was driving his sister's car, and he'd been following me. I parked my car, and he pulled up next to me and said, 'I really wish you wouldn't do this, but if you have to, go ahead. I'll be waiting at home so we can talk.' Then he drove off. So, what could I do? I couldn't just go up there and screw that man, especially with my boyfriend knowing that was what I was doing. So I went on home.

"Well, after that I knew for sure my boyfriend and I needed to break up because there was no reason for me to be sneaking around screwing another man while I was single. It was obvious this relationship was going nowhere fast. After we broke up, he moved in with a woman who lived right down the street from me and married her a month later. And he had me believing he loved me so much."

Miss Nora, sixty-something "I'm going to tell it to you straight," Miss Nora stated. "I once dated a married man. It was about two years after my first divorce. I'd always told myself that I was only going to see him until the right man came along and I meant that. When we first started being together, we'd see each other every day. Eventually every day changed to two or three times a week. Then it was once a week until finally he just started calling me a few hours before he got off work talking about, 'I want to come by but I can't stay.' I'd tell him he could just keep on going then because he needed to make time for me, not just stop by, have sex, and head on home to his wife.

"It didn't take long for me to find out how stingy he was with his money either. I asked him for a big screen TV for Christmas, and he bought me a 19-inch. I didn't complain. He'd asked me for a gold necklace and I got him one. He opened it, said it wasn't the one he really wanted, wore it for a few minutes, then took it off before he left to go home. When he called the next day, I said, 'Look I asked you for a big screen TV, and you got me a 19-inch, but I didn't say nothing about that. I got you a necklace, and you left it laying here like a piece of garbage. I'll just let somebody else have it.' He was there to pick up that necklace within 30 minutes with his tight ass.

"He'd given me a bracelet one time, and I loved it. I must've shown it off to everybody I could. Once we were all hanging out at the bowling alley with our friends and since it wasn't my turn to bowl I was playing with one of those games where you can grab a stuffed animal with those claw things. And what do you think I saw inside the machine? It was the same exact bracelet he'd given me as a gift. That Negro had won it out of a machine, found a jewelry box, wrapped it up, and gave it to me. My friends must've fell out laughing when they found out. Then I started to think back to all the other things he'd given me. He'd probably won them out of a machine, too, with his cheap ass. When I asked him about it, he didn't deny it. He just shrugged his shoulders. I paid his ass back, though. Remember that gold necklace I'd given him for Christmas? I'd taken it to a jeweler and had a fourteen-carat clasp put on it to make it look real, and the only thing real about it was that clasp! When he called me a few months later and told me the necklace had made his neck turn green, I told him he probably just had bad skin. Cheap bastard!

"He was always lying to me, so I shouldn't have been surprised about anything he did. After all, here he was cheating on his wife with me. He was always telling me he couldn't help me pay for this, or he couldn't help me pay for that because his money was tight. He kept telling me how much his wife wanted a new house, but he wasn't going to buy her one because he was going to leave her. It didn't matter to me whether he left her or not because I'd known from the start that I was just with him until the right man came along.

"Anyway, one day this woman who I thought was a good friend of mine called me and asked if my boyfriend had moved. I said no. He told me he wasn't going to move, so I believed him. She went on to say that she went to the same beauty shop that his wife did and had overheard the wife talking about getting a new house. So, I starting thinking about that and about the phone calls he'd made where I didn't recognize the number on my caller ID and just assumed he was calling from somebody else's house. I decided to drive by his house. When I did I noticed that none of the cars in the driveway looked familiar. The next time I talked to him, I asked, 'Did you move?' He said, 'No.' So I believed him.

"This same so-called friend of mine came by my house a few days later to go shopping with me. She was driving and took a detour through a neighborhood close to the mall and started going real slow as we drove past this beautiful house, and who do you think was standing out in the front yard with his car parked right in the driveway? It was my boyfriend with this fool look on his face. She said, 'I told you he moved.'

"I don't know why he thought he had to lie to me. Needless to say, my friendship with this woman ended over my relationship with this man, even though she was right about him.

"No more than six weeks later another friend of mine called and asked, 'Girl, are you and Jacob still together?' Now, I'd already learned that when somebody asked me that question it wasn't a good sign, so I sat down ready to hear the latest. Come to find out this 18-year-old girl he'd been seeing lived in the same apartment complex as my friend, so I went over there. The apartment had a security gate, but my girlfriend buzzed me in as soon as I drove up, then she showed me where this girl lived. Sure enough, there was his truck, parked right out in front of the apartment. I parked, grabbed my hammer off the front seat, got out of my car, and beat the shit out of his truck. I must've broke every window on the motherfucker and was screaming and cursing up a blue streak. His ass finally came outside and he started cursing, too, because he was in love with that truck.

"Then here come the girl's mama talking about, 'Why don't you leave him and my daughter alone. He don't want you.' I told her that this was between him and me and I didn't have anything to say to her or her daughter. I can't stand it when a woman tries to put another woman at fault, like a man can't do no wrong. She didn't need to talk to me. She needed to talk to him, just like I was trying to. I finally calmed down and he left with me. Everything was fine afterwards, except I didn't trust his ass as far as I could throw it.

"When no more than a few weeks later that same girl called and told me he was still seeing her, I was through. I said, 'Okay I'll fix this.' I had her come over to my place an hour before he was supposed to be there so we could talk about it. When he finally got there I made her hide in the closet and told him to go take a bath, that his dinner was nearly ready. He went into the bedroom, stripped and was about to walk into the bathroom when she came out of the bedroom closet. You should've seen his face! I said, 'I thought you told me you weren't seeing her anymore.' I had my knife and planned to use it until she got scared and got in my way when I was trying to get at him. He hurried up and got dressed and left my house with her stupid ass following right along behind him.

"Later, he called me and said he wanted to talk, but I said, 'Hell no!' When he called back and asked if he could come get some of his things, I said 'Hell no, motherfucker, you must be crazy!' He came by anyway and stood outside my door, talking all loud and shit, until I told him I was going to call the police. He kept talking crazy, so to shut him up I let him come in, told him to hurry and get his shit because I'd called the police, but he insisted on standing there and arguing. Then he finally went outside, took his gun out of the truck, and started waving it around. The gun is never loaded. I know because I've known his ass so long, but apparently he's forgotten I know this, and sure enough the police drove up and took him to jail.

"You know that Negro had the nerve to call me and ask me to bail him out? I told him, 'No. Call that bitch you been screwing.' He said, 'I did. She don't have no money.' And I thought, you sorry bastard, that's just what you get. That bitch never did have anything to offer you but what was between her legs, and now when you really need something that matters she can't help you. Well, I bailed him out. I did do that, but I was through with him once and for all. Here it is years later, and do you know that man still calls me every year on my birthday and Christmas? He finally realized it was his loss, but that's too bad."

Sadie, fifty-something

"I've had several affairs, but I never fell in love with any of them." Sadie was, as usual, straight to the point. "Girl, that coffee isn't gonna' fill you up." She motioned to a waiter and had him bring us a platter of tuna sandwiches and some fruit. He was back with it in less than five minutes. I guess when you're the boss you get service like that.

"I'm not the type of woman to stay in an affair too long because I get bored too easy. The longest affair I had lasted two or three years, and that's a long time because it can start interfering with your married life. If you stay in an affair too long, you start comparing one man with the other and that's when you think about leaving home.

"An affair that lasts three or four months is the best kind. You don't put your heart into it, just enjoy it, and move on. Let him know you're only in it because something is missing at home, you don't have any plans of leaving home, and you don't have any plans for him leaving his wife if he has one. Really, it's better if you have an affair with somebody who's married because if a man is single, he's probably out there screwing plenty of other folks and you never know who's watching. If he happens to be in a relationship with a single woman who really wants to make your life miserable, you can best believe she'll call your husband if she finds out that her man is seeing you and you're married. You've got to watch out for all that."

 *Veronica, thirty-something* "I've had one affair and my husband found out about it. Seems like the shit always comes back around." Veronica drank down some of her red soda and licked her lips. "I know it's a stereotype, but I don't care. I love Big Red soda, but I guess that's okay to admit since I can't stand fried chicken."

My eyes roved over all of that other fried stuff on her plate, but I kept my mouth shut.

"I had the affair a year or so after we'd been married. I was in the military and got an overseas assignment. He was supposed to go with me, but he got this well-paying job so he couldn't. We thought we could handle it since the assignment was only for a year."

Veronica picked up the tartar sauce, looked at me, put it back down, and decided to squeeze lemon juice over her fish instead.

"When I got to Germany I started going to church. I hadn't been a frequent churchgoing person at home, and by that I mean I might have gone to church once every other month or so, but I wasn't the kind of person who was in church for Sunday school, teacher's meeting, usher board meeting and all that. I was just a plain old bench member, but I'd been brought up in the church so I knew right from wrong, which is why I was trying my best to be a faithful wife.

"I started going to church every Sunday, but I've got to tell you, when you're not having sex on a regular basis and you've been used to getting it, there's this hormonal problem. I think it's called horniness, and I got a bad case of it about six weeks after I hit German soil. There was this guy living in my building who I became interested in, and believe me when I tell you this, I'd done everything I could think of to stay away from him. I tried everything from going to the gym every day, to going to church on Sundays. I even stayed away from the NCO club at first because I knew that he and his buddies hung out there every Friday and Saturday night. But there really wasn't anything else to do on that base but go to the club and pick up somebody to spend the night with. Well, unfortunately, after a few weeks of doing without, I hit that club and started chasing him."

Veronica eyed the chocolate cake with something close to love in her eyes, and then picked it up and turned it over face down into the turnip greens that she was through eating. "There now, I'm no longer tempted. See, I do have willpower when I want to, but at that time in Germany I didn't have any.

"One night some friends I'd met had a party with food, wine, good music, and fine men as far as the eye could see. Of course, the object of my lustful affection was there because whenever there was a party all the people in our age group would show up. Like I said before, there wasn't that much else to do. A party was always a big event, even though the same faces were always there. I knew this guy liked me because he was always checking me out, and I made it clear that I liked him because I was forever staring at him. One of my co-workers told me I should stop being so forward, but I figured she was just jealous because she'd dated him before I got to the base, but it didn't work out."

"'Damn, why don't you go over and give him a table dance or something?' She was acting real shitty as she tossed her fake-ass weave over her shoulders. 'You acting slutty enough. I thought you was supposed to be married, but you sure ain't acting like it.' I just ignored the hell out of her and when he finally got up from his table and crossed the room to ask me for a dance instead of her, she called me a bitch and walked off.

"We left that party together and after that we were a couple the whole time I was in Germany. But it was no secret to him that I was married, so he and I were both adulterers.

"My husband found out about the affair because that jealous-ass, weave-wearing co-worker of mine wrote and told him about it. When he and I got together she got pissed off at the both of us and felt like she didn't have anything to lose by writing to my husband. I didn't even know she'd written to him until I got back to the States."

Veronica finished off the rest of her soda, then picked up her water and sipped it with much less satisfaction.

"My husband waited about two weeks after I came back home before he asked me if what the letter said was true. I confessed to it because I figured he'd probably done just as much as I had if not more. I knew how horny he could be, and there was no way he would've gone for a year without having sex. After I told him the truth, I told him if he wanted a divorce that was fine with me. I've always been a very secure woman and always felt like I could get another man. I was young, the house was in my name, and I made enough money to pay the bills, so I wasn't really worried. We didn't have a lot of time invested in the relationship. We didn't have children, and we hadn't even lived together for a whole year yet.

"Although he never confessed to his own transgressions I know he had somebody else because he changed the phone number right before I moved back home. Shit, that was a sign in itself. Then some woman left a note in the mailbox for him that said, 'You changed the number. I can't get through to you.' So I knew he'd done his dirt, but he didn't confess to shit. She finally got up the nerve to come over and find out what was going on, but when I answered the door and asked her in, she was so shocked she just turned around and walked off.

"I don't think I could have another affair because there's too much baggage that comes along with it. Now that I have children I think I'd be too tired to deal with anything like that. Besides, right now I'm pretty content."

Cassidy, forty-something "I recently had an affair, but I wasn't looking for it." Cassidy had lowered her voice by now. She didn't want anybody listening in on this. "I know, I know, everybody that has an affair uses that tired line. It started with a conversation, and some of the things we shared were things I'd been missing and needed to hear. He said all the right things. We'd just sit there and talk, and he couldn't believe some of the things I'd tell him about my marriage because some of same things had happened to him.

"He's the exact opposite of what I'd normally be attracted to, but the things he said are what turned me on because for a woman, it's more than the sex. It's what a man says to her and how he treats her. Men mess up when they try to make love to a woman's body without making love to her mind, and once a man marries you he thinks he doesn't have to do that anymore.

"I care for this other man, but I don't love him. I could love him, but I think I'm just having fun playing right now. We've only had sex two or three times and each time it was planned. I was a little nervous the first time we got together, but once I got there everything just sort of naturally flowed. The first time wasn't even at his place; it was at our office building. It was late at night after everybody had left for the evening. We were on the eighth floor of the building and all of the lights in the conference room were out, but the blinds were open so we could see the whole city lit up in front of and beneath us.

"He had me turn to face the window and took me from behind. He didn't even give me time to remove my pantyhose. He just ripped the fabric at the crotch, pushed my panties aside and entered me, and after a few minutes I had the most intense orgasm in my life.

"After that episode he kind of cooled off towards me, so I thought, 'Okay, he wants to play the hit and run thing.' So I pulled back and quit calling and e-mailing him. That next week we ended up having sex on the conference room table, and afterwards he told me he'd decided to cool it because I was becoming too needy. I wish he would've told me that sooner because I would've tried to play it cool, and I wouldn't have been so freaky. But you know how men are. Instead of coming out and telling you why they're acting the way they act, they want to play with you and make you figure it out.

"I guess it was a good thing he decided to back off because I probably would've gotten too attached if I'd let myself go more than I already had. He'd asked me if I'd be interested in having sex with him and another man and I was actually thinking about doing it until he pulled away from me the way he did. I finally decided that since he's single and I'm married and I can't even try to compete with his girlfriend, I might as well leave well enough alone.

"If I had to give a reason why I chose to have an affair in the first place, what made me take the chance, I'd have to say it was what he said to me. He said all the things I wanted to hear, and he did all the freaky shit I wanted to do. It was worth it to me, and yes, I'd do it again."

Giovanni, forty-something "When I first got married, I met this woman who was a few years older than me and already on her second marriage. She was probably no more than 30." Giovanni propped her feet up on the teakwood table in front of her. "We were talking one day, and she told me that she'd had an affair during her first marriage. At that time I was naive to the fact that people actually had affairs in real life. I thought that kind of stuff only happened in books and movies, so I asked her how she could do something like that.

" 'You know what, sweetie?' she replied. 'The man I was having an affair with was the only thing that kept me coming home because it wasn't long into my marriage that I discovered that marriage is not all it's cut out to be. You've got bills that don't get paid on time, or maybe the baby's keeping you up at night. That shit gets hard. But if you're smart, you'll realize that home is permanent. Me and my husband might argue, but in the end I know he's going to be there for me. I had some good sex with my lover and we could talk about anything under the sun, but he could also walk off tomorrow and I'd never see him again. An affair is just a fantasy. It's what you wish your marriage could be.' "

Marcella, forty-something "Affair?" Marcella looked at me like I'd just lost my mind asking her a question like that. "If I'm married and see another man I want to be with, then I shouldn't be with my husband, not if that's what I feel. Why do you want to stay with your husband if you want to be with another man? I don't understand that. There are lots of times you don't want to make love with your husband, but if you don't do it somebody else will.

"I was talking to a friend the other day and she said, 'All my husband wants to do is have sex.' I said to her, 'Well, what else is he going to want? Why not? He gives you everything. He does everything for you, and if he ever finds somebody else that wants to have sex as much as he does, he's going to leave you!'

"Have you ever read that book about why men cheat? What was the main reason? Sex! I understand that not having sex as often as he wants to is no reason for him to mess around, but listen, he cannot help himself. This friend of mine will only have sex with her husband once a month, maybe. I'm not saying you have to do it every day or every time you turn around. I'm talking about casual sex with your husband. You're supposed to do that. If you're married to an old man, that's different. But if you're young and your man is young, isn't that nature?

"If you're married and your husband is pleasing you in almost every way, he's treating you nice, he's not treating you like a slut, he's very courteous and considerate of you, you should be thankful.

"And he shouldn't have to buy for you in order to get sex. There's more to marriage than just buying somebody something. I get so tired of, 'Give me this; it's my birthday.' 'What are you giving me? It's my anniversary.' I don't think relationships should be like that.

"With men it always comes back to sex. If you have a husband, I'm not saying you have to screw him every time he comes to bed because there are times when he doesn't want to and you don't want to either. There are very few men who want to every night when both partners are working. But, hello! If he's the one who wants to have sex most of the time and you don't, you should still give in."

 *Sadie, fifty-something* Sadie clicked her tongue and said, "We all know why men have affairs; it's because they're dogs. It's in their nature to mess around with more than one woman. Me and my brother talk about everything, and he's told me straight up that one woman is not enough. He said he tried to stay faithful, but it was too hard. As a woman, I have to give it to him because when he was married, no matter how many other women he had, his wife never suspected because he loved his wife and wouldn't allow other women to disrespect her." Sadie shrugged her shoulders and cut her eyes towards me. "I know it sounds strange, but he didn't want anybody else to hurt her even though he was risking hurting her himself if she found out what he was doing.

"Some men may have three or four women, and they do it because they know they can get away with it. Some of these women know what's going on but stay there and put up with it. The longer you put up with it, the longer he's going to keep on doing it because he feels like he can do anything he wants to. He might go so far as to disrespect you by bringing all of the signs of an affair home because you won't stand up for yourself.

"Now for the women who don't allow it, their husbands will just sneak and have an affair. Either way they're going to do it if they want to. This is why I never say what my husband didn't do or won't do. I've never seen anything and I've never heard about him doing anything, but I'm not going to say he hasn't or that he won't. He might have done it so well that I didn't find out about it, and that's fine. Like I told him, 'As long as you respect my house, don't bring no disease home, and I'm not hearing about it, then you're doing your job. You're respecting me.' But that doesn't mean I'm telling him to go out and screw around as long as I don't find out about it.

"He's asked me what I'd do if I caught him with another woman and I told him, 'I don't know. Let me catch you and then you'll find out. I can't tell you that I'm going to do something, and I can't tell you that I'm not. I won't know how I'm going to react until I catch you, but I might be the type woman who would kill you so don't try me. I guarantee you one thing: If you mess up on me, your day is coming because I'm going to get payback. I believe in payback. If I find out you've been messing around on me, I might not get you back right away. It might be a year later, but when I find somebody who turns me on, it's going to be my turn.'"

Miss Nora, sixty-something "I never had an affair while I was married. I didn't want anybody but him," Miss Nora stated firmly. "Even if I'd wanted to mess around I wouldn't have because I wanted my children to have the same father. A long time ago, there was no such thing as birth control, and men refused to use condoms.

"I'd starch and iron my husband's clothes every day, even going so far as to make the starch! That man would be wearing a clean, pressed uniform every time he set foot out of that house to go to work. Every day I polished his shoes with my own two hands and washed his shoe laces. I took good care of him even though he was abusive.

"Our marriage wasn't a good marriage because there were times when he'd leave home Friday and not come back until two days later. If he got work, he'd bring his whole paycheck home to me. Then he'd leave, and I wouldn't see him again until Sunday night. He'd take about five or six dollars with him; he didn't need too much because he was so handsome that women would buy for him and give to him.

"I stayed with him and took plenty of shit; it was rubbed in my face every day. Women would call my house and some even had the nerve to come by, but I wouldn't question him. Why should I question him?" she asked, raising her hands towards the ceiling. "I knew where he'd been and what he'd been doing. I wasn't crazy.

"When he finally came back home we'd always get into a fight because I refused to make love to him. I wouldn't let him touch me." She clicked her tongue. "What would I look like letting him touch me after he'd been out in the streets all weekend?" She looked in my eyes and got her answer. "That's right, I'd look like a damned fool, and if I would've tried to pull some of the same stuff he was pulling, I would've gotten a black eye and busted lip for my troubles.

"When this man woke up in the morning, he had to have sex. When he went to bed, he had to have sex. And when he got a break at work, he'd come home and want to have sex, and we did, but he still had plenty of affairs. It didn't help that he worked part-time at a cocktail bar. One night, we made love before he went to work and I decided to go down to the bar and surprise him because they were having a party and I very seldom went to any of the parties. When I got there I saw this woman friend of mine sitting in his car. I asked her what was she doing in my husband's car and didn't even give her time to answer before I reached in and dragged her ass out onto the street. He came out of the club, surprised to see me standing over that woman like I was going to kill her. I knew she had only come there because he'd told her to, but to me it didn't make any difference why she was there. I was whipping her ass for coming to my house acting like she was my friend, laughing and grinning up in my face while all the time sleeping with my husband.

"I'll never forget that night. I was wearing one of my prettiest dresses and my best wig, and I fought her right there in the street. We were fighting like crazy people, rolling around on the street and everything. When we got through she was so raggedy she had to go home, but I just dusted off my dress, picked up my wig, put it on, smoothed it down, and walked into that bar like nothing had even happened."

Ruby, forty-something "I've never been the kind of woman to believe that my man is so in love with my ass he'd never even look at another woman." Ruby clicked her tongue. "That's stupid. If he's messed around since we've been married, I can't prove it, and he sure has been smooth about it because he hasn't stopped doing any of the things for me that he's always done. I know he loves me. I know that if I don't know anything else, but that doesn't mean he isn't going to mess around. He's only human. I just don't want it to be in my face.

"The only thing I have to say is you don't get messy if you're going to do something like that. It's all about respect. If your spouse finds out you're messing around, the trust will be gone and when that happens, what's the point of staying together? I don't want to be wondering where my man is every time he's out of my sight, and I damn sure don't want him checking up on me every five minutes.

Sadie, fifty-something "My husband has had plenty of affairs, he was the town stallion when I met him and had women galore." Sadie responded truthfully. "I can never say I've seen him with someone else because he was the type that liked to party by himself. He wouldn't take me with him, but I'd hear things. I was never able to catch him, and when I'd ask him about it he would deny it. Women called our house all the time and hung up on me. One woman even called and told me that the reason he wasn't home with me one night was because he was with her. I just calmly asked, 'Well, who are you darlin'?' She said, 'His woman.' And I could tell she was surprised that I hadn't gone off on her. I simply replied, 'Well, that's fine because I'm his wife,' and she slammed the phone down in my ear.

"I can be pretty cool 'cause I'm a bitch myself, and it takes a bitch to know a bitch. So whenever somebody called me and asked, 'Is Maurice there?' I'd just say 'No darlin', but this is his wife, can I help you?' The bold ones would keep on and say something like, 'No, I need to speak with him . . . ' and I'd be just as bold and respond, 'Well, darlin' he's not here. He's out in the streets. Check that club over at so and so. You'll probably find him there.' I wouldn't go off on the phone, but I'd cuss his ass out good when he got home. I'd never get mad at the woman on the phone; don't ever do that. If you get mad and ask her, 'Who the hell are you, goddamnit,' she'll know you're having problems at home and that you're insecure. Just be cool, calm and collected and say 'Well, darlin', I'm sorry he's not here to talk to you, but he'll be home shortly. He's here every night; is there a message I can pass on to him in case you miss him?' You have got to keep your cool, and that way she'll start thinking, 'That bitch is happy. I don't care what he's telling me about wanting to leave his wife. That man is taking care of that woman.'

"The last time my husband had an affair, I found out about it and I told him, 'You've got to be the stupidest man in the world to have let me find out!' I think he messed around because he was trying to prove something to himself because he'd gone out drinking and didn't come home all night long. When I woke up and noticed he hadn't come home I got worried because it wasn't something he'd normally do. When he finally came home it was 7:00 in the morning and he was drunk and smelling like sex because he hadn't even taken the time to shower. I said, 'Where in the hell have you been?' He said, 'Out gambling. Shit, I'm going to sleep. I'm tired.'

"When he went to bed I went through his pockets and found some matches with the name of a motel on it, so I called the number and asked for my husband. The person at the other end of the phone said, 'I'm sorry ma'am, but he's already checked out.' I hung up the phone and thought, how stupid could you be to use your real name at a motel.

"He still won't talk about it, and it's been over ten years ago. If I bring it up, he'll get fighting mad and leave because he knows I know what happened. He'd taken some whore to that motel room and I don't know what all they did, but I do know that she stole every dime he had. I think she got him drunk and when he went to sleep she took everything he had because when he came home he didn't have a penny in his pocket, and his leather jacket was missing. When I asked him about the jacket he said he was drunk when he went to this gambling shack and that somebody stole it when he hung it up. He sticks to that story to this day, but he hasn't set foot in a club since it happened."

Giovanni, forty-something "This guy that I'd been seeing off and on, more off than on, finally asked me when I was going to come over and cook for him. I could have jumped for joy when he asked me, but I just played it cool and said something simple like, 'Sure, what would you like me to cook?'" Giovanni rolled her eyes, ashamed of what she was about to confess.

"Well, he told me that he liked fish and asked me to come over to his place to fry him some fish. And, oh, by the way, I just happen to be one of the best fish fryers this side of the Mississippi.

"Well, child, that Thursday evening I bought some fresh fish, took it home and put it in my freezer and the next morning I took it out and carried it to work with me. I didn't want my staff to see it and start asking questions, so I'd wrapped it in plastic, put it inside a brown paper bag and stuck it in the refrigerator at work so it would be thawed out by the time I got off. Girl, I kept waiting for him to call me and let me know what time to come over, but he never did call. And there I was wondering what happened and what I was going to do with all that fish thawing out in the refrigerator.

"By the end of the day, I was pissed—not because of the fish I had spent money on, but because I wanted to see him. I must've called his number thirty times between noon and 6:00 and he never did answer. I stayed late after work, waiting for everybody else to go home before I dragged all that damn fish out of the refrigerator. It was well thawed out by then and I should've thrown it out right then, but no. I was still hoping that he'd call. I wanted to think he'd just misplaced my number or something, but I knew that wasn't the case. And I couldn't take the fish home because my husband didn't even eat fish, so I never cooked it for him."

Giovanni got up and started to pace. "I was so mad I didn't know what to do. I had all this damn fish, and the Negro didn't even try to call me and lie or nothing."

"Well, I finally got him on the phone after probably the fiftieth try at 7:00 P.M. I'd set him up on speed dial because my finger was sore from dialing his number over and over.

"I told him I'd been calling him all day, and you know what he had the nerve to ask me?" Giovanni paused dramatically. "He asked, 'What are you calling me for?' Can you believe that shit? Those were his exact words. I'm sure the only reason he finally answered the phone was because he was tired of listening to it ring.

"I said, 'Didn't you ask me to come over tonight and cook for you?' I knew I hadn't completely lost my mind and imagined the conversation. I had wanted to see him, but not so badly that I'd dream the shit up, but you know how a brother can make you second-guess yourself.

"So he said, 'I told you . . .' now notice he didn't use the word ask. He said, 'I told you I wanted you to come over and cook for me, but I didn't say I wanted it to be this Friday. If I had known you was gonna make such a big deal out of cooking for me, I wouldn't have asked you to do it in the first place.' Now, this Negro was acting like he was doing me a favor to let me buy the food, bring it to him, and stand over a hot-ass stove and cook it for him. And to top it all off I had planned to give him some after I fed him. Baby, I proceeded to tell him exactly what I thought about his selfish, inconsiderate ass and slammed the phone down so hard I was hoping I busted his eardrum. To this day, every time I think about fried fish, I get pissed off all over again."

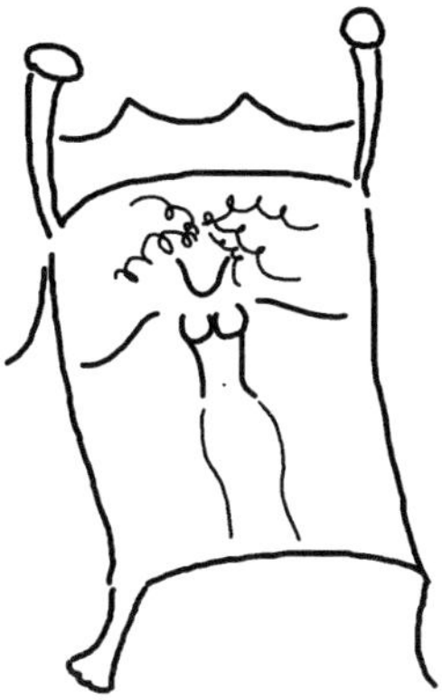

SEX

sex (seks) noun

The sexual urge or instinct as it manifests itself in behavior.
Sexual intercourse.

First Time

Most Erotic

How Many?

Having Sex vs. Making Love

Oral/Anal

Oral, anal, missionary, you name it—it's been done, and we asked about it. We found that some women like hard, wild sex, while others like soft, sweet sex. Some of them have slept with many men, while others have slept with one, maybe two and no one seemed to feel ashamed of how ever many partners they've had or not had. We asked women about the best and worst lovers, the most erotic sex they've had, and all the other intimate things we women share with each other.

"Sex is an emotion in motion."
—*Mae West, 1965*

"Men would always rather be made love to than talked at."
—*Dorothy M. Richardson*

"Aren't women prudes if they don't and prostitutes if they do?"
—*Kate Millett*

"Whether a pretty woman grants or withholds her favors, she always likes to be asked for them."
—*Ibid*

"You mustn't force sex to do the work of love or love to do the work of sex."
—*Mary McCarthy*

"I don't know what I am, darling, I've tried several varieties of sex. The conventional position makes me claustrophobic, and the others give me either stiff neck or lockjaw!"
—*Tallulah Bankhead*

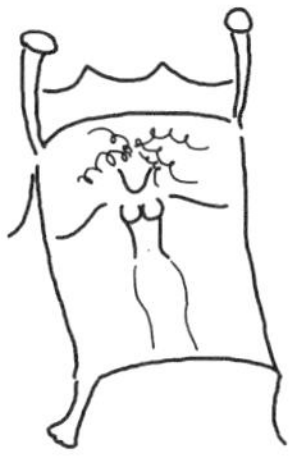

First Time

Miss Charsie, fifty-something Looks are deceiving. At least that was my first thought when this lady I've known most of my life started talking to me about her sexual experiences. I didn't really think interviewing Miss Charsie would be any fun because she was my best friend's mother, and seeing how she'd been so strict on her when we were teenagers, I just knew she didn't have sex, let alone talk about it. When I walked in, she greeted me with her usual peck on the cheek, and then stood back and looked at me. "My Lord, it's been years since I saw you, girl," she said, "And you're cute as you want to be."

"Thank you, Miss Charsie, but you're the one who looks good. You haven't aged a bit. You still look just like you did when we were in high school," I replied.

"Child, stop lying. You know I've got that grandbaby now. If I'm not aging it must be because he makes me move around and use muscles I didn't even know I had. That boy is a mess, just like his mama. By the way, she's working on another one, did you know that? I told her she'd better slow down and wait for you, but I guess you're too busy writing to be bothered, aren't you?"

"Yes, ma'am, I am too busy right now. You and Mama used to tell us we could have babies when we couldn't do nothing else," I reminded her.

"Well, that's good. Just don't wait until you get too old. These babies nowadays can run circles around the parents. What's this book going to be about?" she asked.

After I explained all the details to Miss Charsie, she was too happy to talk. She was still a pretty woman, even after all these years. Her hair hung past her shoulders, but she always had it pinned up, and she still wore those horned rimmed glasses. I'd often wondered if she ever really "let her hair down." But after we got into the interview, I was shocked when she began to talk so freely.

"When I first had sex I was 19," she began. "I waited what seemed to be a hundred years and was dumb as anything because parents didn't explain things back then. They'd say, 'Don't get pregnant!' which was fine, but they didn't tell us how to prevent it. My mother didn't discuss sex with me because she was too embarrassed. I can still remember when her younger sister got pregnant out of wedlock. Everybody was whispering, 'She was messing with those boys.' I was like, 'Messing with boys? What does that mean?' I'd kissed boys and nothing had happened to me, so something must've been wrong with her sister.

"Just to give you an example of how dumb I really was: When I was a girl you didn't have to participate in gym if you were on your period. You got to sit out on the bench. I hadn't started having periods yet, but every week when one of my girlfriends would be sitting on the bench, I'd sit there with her. I'd sit on the bench with a different friend every week. They finally said, 'Girl, you need to go and get checked out because you're bleeding every week.' I knew why they were sitting on the bench, and I wanted to sit there with them because they were my friends. But I didn't realize you only had a period once a month because mine hadn't started yet. I thought I was really fooling that gym teacher.

"When it did start, I was 18 and so ignorant, I ran all the way home thinking, *My mom is going to kill me. She's just going to kill me because she's going to say I was messing with those boys.* I was scared to death because I didn't know what was going on.

"In school they used to separate the girls from the boys while they talked about the menstrual cycle, and I used to slip out of class because I thought only fast girls menstruated. The boys would be out on the playground, and I'd go out there with them because I didn't feel I needed to learn about menstruating since I hadn't started yet. Even when I was married and got pregnant, I didn't really know I was pregnant because my periods never came regularly, and my stupid doctor said I probably couldn't conceive because I was so irregular. You know doctors weren't as knowledgeable back in the '50s and '60s as they are now. My period would come for two months, and then I might not see anything for four months. Then it might come for four months and on the fifth month, nothing. Well, one time I hadn't seen my period for June, July, August, or September, and when I went to the doctor with this bad cold in October he said I was pregnant.

"He asked, 'When is the last time you had a period?'

"I don't know. I think the month before last." I couldn't even remember because it hadn't been important. "I don't mark the calendar because it never comes regularly."

"'Well,' he paused looking at me real crazy, 'You're pregnant.'

"Oh, no. My doctor back at home said I can't conceive. I don't want to hear that garbage.

"'Well, you might not want to hear it, but you are pregnant.'

"'Well, I'll tell you what. My husband and I just ordered a new Cadillac, so I can't be pregnant because that's what I'm going to spend my money on!'

"'You know what? That Cadillac can go back, or you can cancel your order, but there's only one way out for this baby.'

"We went back and forth, and I kept telling him he was wrong because he was young, and I didn't think he knew what he was talking about. I finally told him, 'Listen. You're young, and I think you're trying to experiment on me because I know I can't conceive.'

"He finally stood up, got right in my face and said, 'Lady, you are pregnant. Now you might as well accept it and make an appointment to see your gynecologist because I'm not going to argue with you anymore.'

"I sat there for a moment, dazed, then finally gathered myself and walked out. I made an appointment to see the gynecologist that next week, and when he confirmed that I was indeed pregnant, I was ecstatic. I wasn't trying to get pregnant, but then I wasn't trying not to either.

"Nowadays, there's no excuse. When girls get pregnant, it's usually because they want to. I have a grand-niece who just had her second baby at 17. I told her she needs to do something because there's no reason for that. Sex is wonderful, but you don't have to be stupid just because it's good."

Erica, thirty-something "My first sexual encounter was awful. I was 17 and it was with this guy I'd met while playing tennis. We'd gone to a party together and left to go to the store to get some ice and beer. But first, he needed to go by his friend's house to pick him up, right? And of course this friend wasn't home. Now, the sex wasn't forced because I was curious to find out what it was like, but I didn't think it would go as far as it did. He came before he completely entered me, and I was grossed out. I'd heard about sex, but I guess I hadn't heard everything because I thought his semen just felt nasty. I felt like I'd been drenched in slime and was mad at myself because I didn't even like him that much. I was really only with him because I thought he was cute. I really didn't intend to have sex with him.

"Since that time, I've been with about eleven men. I'm not ashamed of that because at one time in my life I was kind of wild. I used to think like a man. I was like, 'Hey, I'm out to have a good time. I ain't trying to date or marry you.' I'll have to admit, I used to be a dog. But once I had my fill of men and found that most of them were just about the same, I calmed down and changed my ways."

Sadie, fifty-something "The first time I had sex it was terrible, terrible, terrible!" said Sadie. "Back in my day, you couldn't even go out with a young man unless his parents knew your parents and both sides agreed it was okay. This young man I was dating took me to the movies and when he brought me home, we decided we'd kiss in the car where no one could see us. That was nothing new. We'd always done serious petting and stuff, but this one time it got too hot and heavy, and he wouldn't stop. I guess you'd call it date rape nowadays but back then, you'd get accused of being a 'little fast wench' if you told anybody what happened, so I knew I couldn't tell anyone.

"After that I didn't like him anymore because I felt so hurt and violated. He literally tore my panties off and screwed me so hard I could hardly walk into the house. That's just not the way a girl should lose her virginity.

"If my daddy would've caught him with me in that car or found out about it later he would've killed him, so I never told anybody. I talked to him after that, but we never mentioned what had happened. As a matter of fact, this is the first time I've ever mentioned it to anybody."

Nikki, fifty-something "I started masturbating when I was in the 7th grade. That's when I found out I had a vagina. By the time I was 16, I was ready to know what it was all about. I had been feeling around down there and I knew what made me feel good, so I started doing it on a regular basis. When I had sex for the first time, I was disappointed because he didn't make me feel the way I felt when I did it by myself. I was waiting for the whistles and streamers and firecrackers to go off, but when they didn't, I asked, 'Is that it?!' "

Isis, twenty-something "I know it's hard to believe, but the first time I had sex I was in the 10th grade, and I got pregnant. I was a straight-A student, the only child, and my parents had high hopes that I would be the first child in their family to go to college, so, of course, they were very disappointed. The bad things is, the sex wasn't even what I expected it to be. That's why young people need to wait. Since that first time when I was 15 years old, I've had sex with three men and I guess I haven't found a 'best' one yet because I still don't think sex is such a big deal."

Marcella, forty-something "My first sexual encounter was with my son's father," Marcella said looking disappointed. I was 19, going on 20, and I was so scared because Mommy always told us that sex was bad; therefore, I didn't enjoy it. I didn't start enjoying it until I was about 23 or 24 years old. Really, because it had always been put in my head as something bad by my mommy as well as other women on the island where I lived. After we had sex I felt so guilty, I couldn't face nobody. I was very depressed because I'd been taught that good girls don't do that, and you go to hell if you do.

"I've had sex with a total of six men now and the last time was nine months ago, but that doesn't bother me. I'm not gonna ruin my life behind sex. I've had a lot of opportunities, but I'm not gonna have sex just to be doing something. I wouldn't do that. I don't want to be with somebody who already got somebody. I want to be with somebody who don't have nobody but me. Even if he has somebody but they're not together, I'd rather be alone, because I don't believe in sharing a man.

"I work, I go to aerobics, and when I come home I'm sewing, baking, or doing something else, so it don't bother me to be alone. On Saturdays, me and my girlfriend do a lot together. We either go out or we go to all the carnivals. Next weekend we're going to Houston for a carnival. We've been back to Trinidad together twice, and last month we went to Carnival in Miami.

"So, I really don't have time to be sitting around worrying about sex. Life has too much other stuff to offer for me to worry about that."

Celeste, fifty-something "The first time I had sex I was 18 years old. It had to be sex. You couldn't call what we did making love because he tore my clothes off. He was several years older than me and was supposed to be taking me to meet his aunt. His aunt still hasn't shown up, and that was 37 years ago. When he was through, he took me to my older sister's house and told her some girls had jumped on me.

"My mother had always said, 'Girls, just keep your dress down,' and that's what I was trying to do, but he kept kissing me and pulling on my clothes until he got them off. The next thing you know, I was pregnant, and that was from my first sexual encounter. I think I was 21 or 22 and married before I made love for the first time."

Bianca, thirty-something "I just had my first orgasm with a man last year, and I'm in my early thirties. I thought something might be wrong with me, so I asked my mother. I can talk to her about everything. She told me, 'Bianca, baby, some women never reach an orgasm and some women don't reach them until they get older because it's not always easy to have an orgasm with a man. If his body isn't touching yours in exactly the right spot at exactly the right time, it just doesn't happen and most men don't even know when and where to touch you. That's why you have to tell them most of the time.'

"I was so disappointed to hear that because I think that's why some women don't want to have sex. The men are getting all the thrills! They do all this talking like they know so much about our bodies, but without instructions, most of them couldn't make a woman have an orgasm if you paid them.

"I even talked to my doctor about it and told her it was hard for me to have an orgasm during intercourse. She said that a lot of times, because women are doing so much these days, when they have sex their body is there but their mind isn't, so it's hard for them to relax enough to have an orgasm. She said a woman's clitoris is very much connected to her mind.

If the two don't connect, and your man is not moving in the right spot, you're not going to get yours.

"Now that would be a good subject for a book. But you know men hate to ask for directions, so they probably wouldn't even read it."

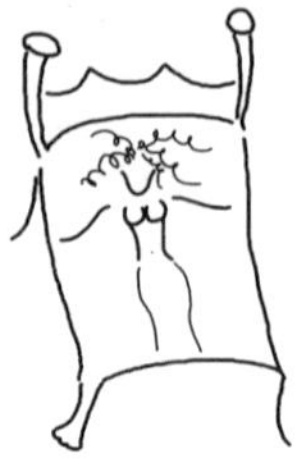

Most Erotic

Porsche, forty-something "I've told my boyfriend so many things about me that I know he wouldn't want to be with me on a permanent basis," said Porsche sipping on her wine. "I even told him about the time I pledged with my sorority. Don't look at me like that. I know I'm not supposed to reveal my sorority secrets but that was so long ago.

"One of the things we had to do to prove our sisterhood was make love with another woman." I guess the shock was all over my face because Porsche bucked her eyes at me mockingly, even though she didn't appear to be embarrassed at all. "Yes, I've been with women just like I've been with men and I'm not saying I enjoyed the experience, but I've done it. They told us we were supposed to love our line sisters the way we loved ourselves, but in hindsight I think they were just being freaky because they knew they could get away with it. I'm not a lesbian or anything; it was just part of hell week. The whole line participated. It was one big female orgy."

"Girl, how in the world did you bring yourself to do that?" I asked in disbelief. "I know how much you love men. I can't even imagine you getting with another female."

"Well, we all got high first, so there was no emotion involved, just pure sex. I didn't touch anybody's coochie, but I saw others who did. I remember kissing and massaging my roommate's breasts and we both got a real rush from that, but that's as far as it went for me. All I can say from that experience is that you shouldn't knock anything before you try it. When I did tell my boyfriend about it he wasn't even shocked. All he said was, 'Damn, I wish I could've seen that! Maybe I should call your old roommate up and find out a few more ways to please you.'

"See, that's the reason I don't have time for no man under 30. Think about it. Even if it's just a plain old physical relationship, most men between the age of 21 and 30 haven't realized that they're in it to please you. They're still in it to please themselves. You get a man who's about 35 or older, he's already learned that his dick don't get as hard as he'd like it to get, and when it does it don't stay that way all night, so he's in it to please you."

Eboni, forty-something "Me and a guy I was seeing were on our way home from a dance one night when all of a sudden it started to storm. Now, I don't know what it is, but for some reason thunder, lightning, and hard rain make me feel sexy." Eboni paused for emphasis, crossing her legs. "So, we drove to a secluded area, parked, and started to make love, but I felt like I just wasn't getting all of him like I wanted to. I said, 'Forget this! Let's get out of the car.'"

"Eboni, no you didn't."

"Honey, yes I did. I came out of my dress, kicked off my heels, and we got out there in the rain, buck naked on the side of the road. My feet were muddy and my hair was soaking wet, but I had a fresh perm so I wasn't worried. I got on my knees and took care of business, then he put me on the hood of the car and we screwed for a while in all that rain. It passed through my mind that the police or anybody could catch us out there, but it was so good I didn't give a damn. That was the best come I ever had."

"It's a wonder you didn't catch pneumonia," I said.

"I didn't get pneumonia, but I did catch a cold that had me coughing off and on for a week. I swear, every time I coughed it made me think about how good that brother was banging me on top of his hood and I got horny all over again."

Giovanni, forty-something "Growing up in a family that had lots of money, I always had to be the perfect little lady. I'm originally from Atlanta, and my grandfather owned the first and only chain of black bookstores in town, which he passed down to my father, so my family was well known. The only bad thing about that was I couldn't do anything without my parents finding out, sometimes before I even got home.

"If I wasn't at church I was in charm school or tap dance lessons—always something to do to keep me from doing what I wanted to do. But I also had the benefit of attending an 'all-black' private school, and I received a two-seater Mercedes as a birthday gift when I turned 17. Now that I think back on it, I really couldn't complain. But you know how it is when you're young. You feel like you're being bored to death while the other girls you know are having fun because you're looking from the outside in. I didn't seem to be having much fun at all so I was constantly complaining."

"I wish," I said. "Girl, I can't even afford a Mercedes now and I'm grown. You were very lucky to have parents who were able to give you so much. They must have trusted you or else they wouldn't have given you a Mercedes at 17."

"I guess they trusted me, but by the time my father got through lecturing me on my way out the door, I almost didn't want to go anywhere." Giovanni stood at attention. "To this day I can distinctly hear him saying, 'Giovanni, remember that when you walk out of this house you are representing your family. Don't go out there and do anything that would embarrass us or yourself because if you do people won't ever let you live it down.'

"I always felt like I was living in an aquarium or something, so I really didn't get to have much fun with boys when I was growing up. I vowed that when I left home I was going to do whatever I pleased to make up for all the fun I'd missed as a teenager.

"My first year in college, I decided not to go home for spring break. Me and my girlfriend went to Jamaica instead. Hell, I had the money in my expense account and my parents thought I was going to Cancun with the rest of the college kids, so they didn't complain. Well, we were on the beach hanging out the first night there, and I met the most beautiful man I'd ever seen. He had dark green eyes, skin the color of a caramel apple, and I got hot just listening to him talk.

"So, I decided, that I would try to have sex with him sometime during the next week. This was my chance to do something I never had the opportunity to do: be promiscuous and enjoy it without worrying about someone telling my daddy.

"It turned out he was actually from Jamaica, but had left to attend college in New York, and was home only during spring break himself. His family lived about an hour away from the hotel, but his older brother lived and worked at the hotel, so he was staying with him for the week.

"We sat there on the beach and talked until it was pretty late, and then he asked me if I'd like to come to his brother's room for a drink. At first I was thinking, *I do not know this man, and his brother might be up there waiting for him to bring some innocent girl up there so they can run a train or something. I don't have any business going to his room.* I asked him if he was sure his brother wouldn't mind, but it turned out his brother had just left for work and wouldn't be home until early the next morning. So I gave my girlfriend the room number. She was running her mouth with some guy she'd just met. Off we went to his room with me thinking I was all grown up and that nothing would happen that I couldn't handle.

"By the time we got there, the crotch of my swimsuit was soaked. His brother actually had a suite, which was nice because we could go into the bedroom and close the door. He fixed me a drink, and we'd barely closed the door before he was all over me. He was working his way down my body but I'd been swimming in the ocean, so I didn't feel clean. So he said he'd wash me and we got into the shower and he washed me from head to toe with nothing but soap and his hands. I wanted to pass out it felt so good, but then I got scared because I was thinking, *How could a girl like me be doing something like this? What if my parents found out? Hell, what if his brother walked in on us.*"

"Yeah, and what about AIDS?" I interrupted. "Weren't you worried about catching something from some guy you didn't even know?"

"Wait, girl, let me tell you. After he got through washing me and drying me off, he laid me on the bed and kissed me again. Then he looked right into my eyes and said, 'Relax, I won't do anything you don't want me to do, and I won't go anywhere you don't invite me. But I want you to know I intend to please you completely. If I'm too rough, I want you to stop me, and If I'm not rough enough I want you to tell me. If there's anything you would like me to do, let me know. I don't expect you to do anything other than open yourself up to me unless you absolutely want to. I'll do the rest.'

"All I could do was shake my big head up and down like a dog in a window, and before I could even think of a response he'd slipped on a condom and was already inside me. And I do mean inside me because the brother was filling every spot I had, even the ones I didn't know I had. Even though I should have been nervous, I wasn't because he was kissing me and touching me like he knew me.

"He told me everything I wanted to hear, kissed me everywhere I wanted to be kissed, sucked my fingers, my lips, my earlobes and everything else I had that could be sucked. He must have stayed hard for at least two hours before he finally came. And when he did, he held me and kissed me and said my name, 'Umm, Giovanni . . . Giovanni . . . where did your mama get you from, girl?' Whew! I gotta stop. I'm getting horny just thinking about it."

"I know, I'm looking at you perspiring and all that like it just happened last night. Girl, why didn't you go find that man when you were looking for a husband? It sounds like he was the one."

"Ooh, no! I'd have a house full of babies with a man who makes love like that! He actually did it like it was something he'd studied. I mean, I haven't been with David for 21 years for nothing. He's a great lover. He just doesn't move like that man did. Lord have mercy, I don't know of any other man who moved like that. I wonder where he is now." Giovanni looked up at the ceiling as if her question would be answered from above.

"Wherever he is, he'd better stay there," I said, "because I got a feeling if you saw him again you'd probably go crazy and leave your husband and kids. Was that a one-night thing or did you spend any more time with him while you were there?"

"Oh, I spent every day with him the rest of that week. There was no way he was going to make me feel that good and leave me hanging for five more days. That was the best sex I have ever had, seriously. We tried to stay in touch when we went back to school, but with me in Texas and him in New York, it was just too expensive. We probably wrote and called each other for about six months after we got back to school, but we both had busy schedules and too many other things going on. Somehow we just stopped communicating. I guess it just wasn't meant to be.

"Anyway, I started dating a guy about a week after I got back to school who was really nice and he was a good lover, too. He wasn't no Jamaican, but he was pretty good. Our relationship got pretty serious so I didn't dare go back to Jamaica for spring break that following year because I know I would've got turned out for real. Besides, I didn't need to go back to Jamaica a second time like Stella. I got my groove back the first time I went."

Macy, fifty-something "The most erotic sex I ever had was in a swimming pool at a hotel. Me and my boyfriend were spending the weekend at a little private resort in Palm Springs, and he wanted to go to the pool at about one in the morning when there was no one else around. Now, I'm 50 and he's 38 so you must understand that his energy level is a little higher than mine. I thought we were in for the night after dancing for two hours straight, but he said he wanted to show me something, so I put on my little leopard-print swimsuit, the one I bought especially for this trip, and pranced out to the pool on his arm. Thank God the lights in the pool weren't on.

"When we got in the water, he put his hands underneath me as I floated, and he told me to relax. Then he said, 'Open your eyes and look up at the moon and those beautiful stars, and visualize that there's no one else in the world but you and me. Don't think about anything else but how peaceful and quiet it is out here.' Just listening to him talk while looking at the moon and stars was so soothing I almost went to sleep. He could've dipped my big ass under that water and drowned me I was so relaxed.

"Then, he pulled me toward him and whispered in my ear, 'I'm going to make you feel like you're up there on that moon. Just hold on to me.' I can't even begin to tell you the things he did to me in that pool, but baby, let me tell you, I went to the moon that night and that's no lie."

Jazz, forty-something "Whenever my husband comes home from a business trip, that's when we have our most erotic sex because we usually end up with me on his lap in the car at the airport parking lot. One time we actually did it in the ladies room at a restaurant because I was too hot to wait until we got home."

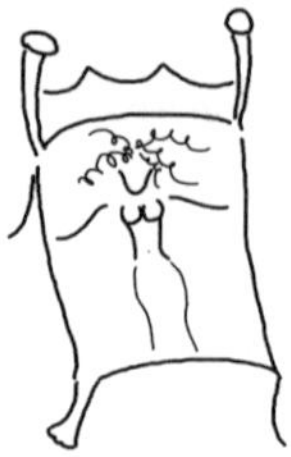

How Many?

Celeste, fifty-something "I've lied so many times about the number of men I've slept with that I can't remember what the truth is! I'm pretty sure it's fourteen. I can say that I've always known their names and I've never had a one-night stand. I don't believe there's anybody out there fine enough to have a one-night stand with."

Cassidy, forty-something One day while sitting under the dryer at the salon, working on my notes for the book, I met Cassidy, who was also sitting under the dryer. Both our beauticians were eating lunch, so we figured we might as well pass the time by talking, and I ended up telling her about the book, since that's what she really wanted to talk about anyway.

"Neat idea," she said. "I'll bet that chapter on sex will be a good one. What kinds of questions did you guys ask for that one?"

"Well, we asked many questions. Like, how many men have you had sex with?"

"What? Ooh, honey, that's going to be good. I'd love to offer some insight on that one if you'd care to hear it."

Always prepared to get a good story, I pulled out my recorder. I'd heard this lady talk before, and she was outspoken and had plenty to say. So there was no reason to pass up the chance for something that might add more flavor.

"Go right ahead," I pointed to the recorder, turning it on. "Tell me how many men you've had sex with."

"Well, let me start by saying I admire a woman who waited until she got married to have sex, and has had sex only with that one man, but I'm not one of those. I learned a lot of things from the men I was with before I got married, and I'm not ashamed of that. I even tell my husband he married me because I'm a good bitch. He's been with me as long as he has because I'm good at what I do."

"You actually say that to him, and he's not offended?" I asked.

"Hell, no. Offended for what? He wasn't no virgin when I met him either, so what can he say? Shit, he's glad I know what to do. It's sad when a woman has been with only one man because women like that are very inexperienced about men and the things men tend to do. Those are the women who get hurt most of the time. Every now and then they might get lucky enough to get a good man who will stick with them and teach them a few things, but more than likely they end up with a man who takes for granted that they're so naive.

"I even had a man tell me one time, 'I know my wife. I'm the only man she's ever been with and she don't know what else is out there. She likes sex, but she won't even think about doing some of the things I want to do, and I like nasty sex every now and then. I know she'll always be there for me, but I keep me a woman on the side so I can get real freaky every now and then.'

"As a matter of fact, the experiences and relationships I had before I got married have helped me to stick with my husband this long. Otherwise, I would've been gone after the first little argument, thinking there might be something better out there. When you've been with a few men, you realize they're all the same in one way or another, and you just learn that they are the way they are and you deal with it. Basically, they all do just about the same thing. Some are rough, some are not rough enough, some are inexperienced, and some know exactly what to do. You just have to find the one you love, and tell him what you want.

"I think its good to have somebody to compare to. A lot of times when a woman has had sex with only one man, she doesn't know the good from the bad and that's how she ends up accepting someone who can't please her. The problem is, if you get into a relationship where the sex is bad, it only gets worse as you get older. If it's just mediocre now, it's definitely going to get worse."

Miss Nora, sixty-something "I've had sex with a lot of men. I can't even count how many. But there were times when I had to close my eyes and grit my teeth because it was all about money and nice things that I needed for me and my children. It sometimes made me sick inside for a man to touch my body because I didn't care for some of them that way. They liked me and did all of these nice things for me, so sometimes I had to produce, but it still made me sick inside to have sex with someone I really didn't care for. Even though they didn't know how I felt, I knew."

India, thirty-something "Let me count. Okay, twelve, I think. I might have missed one, but if I did I guess he didn't leave an impression. Now, I'm not boasting or anything because I don't think that's anything to be proud of. I don't think women, or men for that matter, should be so promiscuous with all the shit out there nowadays. But most of the men I slept with, I slept with before I got married, before AIDS was an issue. I can't say I'm happy that I slept with that many, but at least I can say I had some variety and I know what I like and what it takes to turn me on. Some of them were sorry lovers who didn't know the first thing to do, and some were okay lovers who were just that—okay. I honestly can't say I had more than four out of that twelve who were really good lovers, and that's a shame. I guess the problem with the ones who weren't any good is that they were young and inexperienced. The men who were in their mid-thirties and up were the best lovers because they were patient and they actually made love to me or at least they made it feel that way.

"I remember one fool I was messing with, every time I'd get ready to come, he would raise up looking all crazy and say, 'No, uh uh, not yet,' and move me into a different position. That shit used to piss me off because half the time I would never get back to the point of orgasm before he did, so I wouldn't get mine at all. Stupid-ass fool.

"Let me tell you, when you find a man you really care for and you're compatible in bed, stop looking because most of them don't even know what the hell they're doing. One guy even spit when he was going down on me because he got pubic hair in his mouth. He didn't wipe his mouth on the sheet or try to take the hair off his lip with his fingers. He actually spit. I hear him down there making this noise, but I didn't feel anything so I raised my head to see what he was doing, and the fool was spitting, like he had lint in his mouth or something. I tell you—that took the cake."

Veronica, thirty-something "Veronica, girl, look at your plate. I thought you said you wanted to lose some weight? You got fried fish, fried potatoes, fried squash, and turnip greens—not to mention that big old piece of chocolate cake and Big Red soda you're gonna wash it all down with."

This was the same conversation we always had whenever I went to lunch with Veronica. She's always telling me to help her because she's worried that her husband might stray if she doesn't lose the 65 pounds she's gained since she married him five years ago and had a baby. Veronica wears beautiful, expensive clothes, but she recently had to start shopping at The Avenue, a shop for full-figured women, and she's been depressed ever since. I always tell her that beauty is skin deep, even though her face is getting so round that her eyes look squinty when she laughs. But she listens for a while, gets her self-esteem back, get's a new haircut and starts exercising and dieting, only to fall off the wagon a week later and go on another binge.

"Ooh, you know you're being trifling. I have mirrors at home. I know I need to lose weight. I don't need nobody to tell me that. Besides, I'm not dieting today. I'm having a splurge because I deserve it."

"You deserve it? For what?" I asked. "Aren't you the one who said you needed someone to be accountable to? I'm just trying to help you, sister-girl. That's why we stopped coming here for lunch, remember? All those vegetables they got and you want the fried stuff. Believe me, I know how hard it is. I need to lose some weight myself, but when I get serious, I'm not coming here anymore. I'm going to bring my lunch."

"Whatever. I didn't say I was giving up. I just said I was splurging today, that's all. I don't know if I'll ever have that figure I had when I was 21 anyway. My body hasn't been the same since I had the baby.

"So let's get to this question you asked me, which I still can't believe. If I wasn't so sure I could trust you, I wouldn't even answer. But I know quiet is kept with you, right?"

"You know I'm not trying to tell your business to everybody, girl," I assured her. "But I saw that picture you have on your desk. You know that one you keep to motivate yourself. You must have had all the guys drooling over you back then. Come on, how many men have you had.

Reminisce a little and then maybe you won't want all that food on your plate."

"You heffa!" she replied. "Well, I thought about it on the way here, and I think I've been with thirteen."

"Tell me about the one who you remember most."

"Let me see. One in particular stands out because he was by far the worst. When I was 21, I had sex with this guy who was 18 because he was just crazy about me, and I wanted to blow his mind. I used to really be like that. I liked to impress men, even if I didn't really want them. We'd met at college. He was a freshman living in the dorm, and I had my own apartment because I was a senior. To this day, I still remember getting ready for him to pick me up.

"I showered with Johnson's Baby Bath, put baby oil all over myself before drying off so that my skin would be especially soft, and then put on a cute little tangerine-colored sundress that came only to the top of my thighs. It was summertime so, of course, I didn't wear any panties, and the bra I had on was so sheer, all it did was offer some support and show off what I had to offer. When he got there, I sashayed in front of him while making him a drink, making sure he got a good view of my big pretty legs and the way that dress was hitting my butt, and honey, by the time we got ready to go to dinner, he was ready to eat me instead! I must admit, I'd made myself horny by wearing that dress with no panties, but I had to make him wait, just to ensure my own pleasure.

"We went to dinner and then to a movie and he couldn't keep his hands off my legs. I'd let him get so far, but then I'd stop him. I knew I was driving him crazy, but that was the whole point. When the movie was almost over, I let him get his hand up far enough for him to realize I didn't have any panties on and when he felt the hair on my coochie, he almost jumped out of his seat. I threw my head back and laughed a quiet, sexy little laugh, but I really wanted to laugh out loud. I was so tickled. As soon as the first credit started to roll he had me by the hand, up and out the door, and on our way back to the car. 'Ooh wee,' I thought. 'This is going to be good.' An 18-year-old football player with all that energy, those fine thighs, and big fine hands. I couldn't wait to saddle him up and ride."

"Ooh, you so nasty, Veronica," I interjected.

"That's right, I was being nasty, but it was fun. Anyway, to make a long, long story real short, we got back to my apartment and it was over in five minutes. Yes, that's what I said, five minutes. I was so pissed I could have slapped the shit out of him before he even got off of me. My immediate thought was, *What in the hell was that? You mean I did all that for this?* My mind went back to how he kept grinning while we were eating, and I guess I should have known right then that he was too damn excited to do anything for me. I mean, the boy was packing, but he just couldn't do shit, and I know he was embarrassed to come that fast at his age, but I didn't care about his feelings.

"I was like, 'You have to be at practice at seven in the morning, so I guess you'd better go.' And even though I tried my best to say it nice, I know it didn't sound nice because it was all over my face. Here I was thinking, *I'm gonna show him something tonight*, and I guess if he'd known what he was doing I would've had a chance. But when he went soft after five minutes, the thrill was gone. I wanted to tell him, 'Get your no-screwing ass out of my apartment right now,' but I didn't want to make him feel worse than he already did.

"I learned my lesson that time. Rule of thumb: If a guy is fine as hell, big and strong looking and says all the right things, but his teeth start chattering when you kiss him because he's nervous, leave him the hell alone because you're in for a big disappointment if it goes any further."

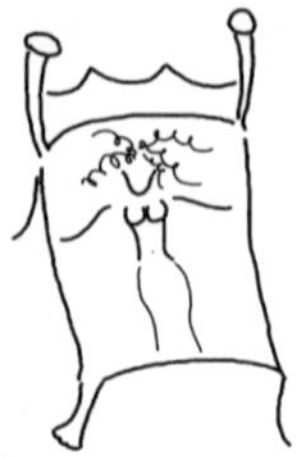

Having Sex vs. Making Love

Ruby, forty-something I thought I'd never have a chance to interview Ruby since she's so busy with her dance studio. We canceled at least three appointments because her schedule kept changing and I was just about ready to give up. When she called me on a Saturday night, saying her husband and son would be at the Dallas Mavericks game for at least four hours that next day, I figured it was now or never, so I canceled my own plans for the afternoon.

I met Ruby about four years ago at the Women's Business Center where we were both taking a class on Women Entrepreneurs, and we instantly hit it off. She was one of the most friendly, positive, and upbeat women I'd ever met, and I really enjoyed talking to her about anything, so I knew interviewing her would be fun because she was just a fun person to be around.

When I arrived, she escorted me to the family room. It was nice and big, with a wall of windows that looked out over a huge yard where a pool was being built for their son who was a freshman in high school. He was already known as one of the finest swimmers in the state and Ruby was so proud of him that she beamed whenever she talked about him.

Her husband is a lawyer, and their story is really poignant in that they met right after college and dated a couple of years before finally getting engaged. Ruby was busy dancing and was on the road often, so Jon didn't want to rush her into anything she'd regret. They'd been married 15 years now, and she seemed to be happy with her life.

As we sat in the den drinking iced tea, I couldn't help but ask, "Will you guys be skinny-dipping out there when that pool is ready?"

"Girl, you know I'm not going skinny-dipping in my own backyard. My neighbors' houses aren't that close, but you know some people are nosey as hell. I don't want nobody to see me back here naked and start watching me every night. We really only got that pool for our son. He's always complaining that he needs to work on his technique, so we figured we'd get our money's worth if we put one in. We even had to have heaters put in the damn thing so he can use it in the winter time. But that Jacuzzi, that's my new toy. That's why it's over there by my bedroom. I can get in, relax, get out, and go to bed."

"Ummhmm. I'm sure you'll get good use out of it if you can slow down long enough. Let me get started so I won't take up all your free time. I know you don't get to have the house to yourself often, so I don't want to stay too long."

"Oh, no girl. You don't have to be in a hurry. We've got at least three hours. I'm a little anxious to see what you're going to ask me, though, so I'm ready if you are."

"Okay, then. I've got lots of questions, but you can start by telling me if you think there's a difference between making love and having sex."

"Of course, there is a difference. Making love starts when you get up in the morning, even if you're not in the same house with that person.

"If they call you to say, 'How are you doing this morning? I just called you to say I was thinking about you and I can't wait to see you tonight,' that means a lot. It sets the mood for how you'll feel when you see him because by the time you get with him you already feel like you're in the mood to make love.

"Making love is a gift two people give to each other, but sometimes when you're married it doesn't seem like that because you don't make the phone calls or leave the little notes like you did at the beginning of the relationship. When you really care deeply for a man you want to give him something that he can't buy—you can't put a price on it. A woman giving her body to a man that she's really in love with is the ultimate gift and it should be the other way around with him giving his body to her as well. There's no gift greater than that. That's the difference between having sex and making love—it's the way you feel about each other and how much you're both willing to give of yourself.

"Now having sex, on the other hand, can be whatever. There doesn't have to be any emotion involved. You can have sex with anybody, no strings attached. You might even just do it because you're attracted to each other and want to see what the other person has to offer.

"The problem is that sometimes people have casual sex and it turns out to be more than they bargained for."

"Give me an example of what you mean," I requested.

"Okay, for instance, when I was engaged to and totally in love with my husband sixteen years ago, he was my best friend and I just knew the sun rose and set on him. One night we had gone to the movies and out to dinner, but the whole time I could just tell that something wasn't right."

She crossed her bare arms and rubbed them like she'd caught a chill. "Most women I know have that sixth sense. I think, whether we want to deal with it or not, we always know when things aren't the way they're supposed to be. Every time I asked him a question I had to repeat myself because he wasn't listening.

"When I asked him what was wrong, he just mumbled something about stress on the job. He was a rising young lawyer, and he's always been an overachiever so I guess that's why he's so successful now. I asked him earlier if he'd spend the night with me since he'd been away for the last week and I was pretty horny, but he declined and gave me some lame excuse about having to be at the office bright and early. He pulled into my driveway, turned off the ignition, and said he had something to tell me. Now, I was sure something was wrong because he could be as sick as a dog and still want to make love. When he wouldn't look me in the eyes I started thinking all kinds of things, like maybe he'd discovered he was gay or maybe he decided he didn't want to be with me anymore, but it wasn't anything like that.

"He started off saying how much he loved me and that he wouldn't want to hurt me for the world, and in the very next breath said he'd gotten another woman pregnant."

Ruby paused like she was reliving the hurt all over again. "Do you know how it feels to be in love with someone and have him tell you some other woman is going to have his baby? I felt like my heart had split in two. He went on to say that the woman was an ex-girlfriend that he'd run into at his college reunion, the same reunion that I couldn't make because I was on the road with my dance group. He told me that it all began with them getting together for old times' sake, and if you ask me, that was his first mistake. Ain't no way you're going to get together with an ex-girlfriend while you're out of town and be surprised when you end up in bed with one another. Of course, he went on to say, as they all do, that the sex meant nothing. But how can sex mean nothing? And if it meant nothing to him with her I had to wonder how soon it would mean nothing to him with me. The sad part was that it truly didn't mean anything to him. She was just something to do at the time, but you could best believe it meant the world to her. Otherwise why would she take the chance of getting pregnant? Once again, another prime example of how differently men and women look at things.

"I don't know about you, but there aren't very many women I know who can sleep with a man and keep it strictly on a sexual basis with no feelings attached. He tried to explain to me that the woman was making a big deal out of nothing and to him it wasn't a big deal until he got caught, because until she called him and told him she was pregnant, he'd forgotten all about that one night. Once Jon told her he was in love with me and had no intention of marrying her, it was too late to abort the baby, so she carried him to full term and gave him to Jon when he was born, saying, 'If I can't have you, then I don't want your son either.'

"I felt our love could handle anything, so I forgave him, married him, and decided to be a mother to his son. It hasn't always been easy, but the things we went through made our marriage stronger. Of course, since that happened, I don't believe in casual sex. It's just not worth it to me.

"I've been married for 14 years and I dated my husband for five years before we got married, so I've been with him for a long time. I hate to say it, but sex for us has become too routine; it feels like a chore. It's not because of me. You can look at me and tell I'm not prudish! When I'm working I love wearing 2-inch heels with my business suits, and when I'm playing I love my mini-skirts and crop tops, and when I'm horny I want to be satisfied.

"I used to enjoy spontaneous, passionate love-making at least three times a week with my husband, but when we haven't spoken any kind words to each other all day and saying only enough to run the house, I can't get in the bed, roll over, and just open my legs. The desire isn't there, so now I guess it's just sex for us.

"I guess men can have sex and not be into it emotionally, but most women can't because we have to make a conscious decision to make love and our emotions are very much involved. Men can get in, come, and be satisfied because they don't have to make a decision, it's usually made for them with their penis.

"To me, making love involves mind and body. I want a man to make love to my mind so I can feel free to scream, grunt, talk dirty, or do whatever turns me on, without worrying if he's thinking, 'Damn, she's a nymph.' I want to feel completely satisfied when we're finished, and I want to be able to make him feel the same way. But it's just too much work when you're not in tune with each other anymore. I truly wish sex could always be exciting like it was when we first started dating, but when he treats me like I'm just there to fulfill a need, I don't even feel like going through the motions."

Miss Nora, sixty-something "I don't remember what sex or making love feels like anymore because it's been so long since I've had any good loving. I wouldn't know what to do if I got some, but it don't bother me to be here alone, because ain't no man getting nothing free from Nora. Uh-uh, baby. He's got to bring some good loving and some cash or credit cards. Now that I think about it, I can't really say that I've ever made love. I honestly can't tell you that. There have been times where the sex has been good and I felt good afterwards, but I just treated it the same way men do because I had needs that I wanted fulfilled."

Macy, fifty-something "I made love with my first husband, but he broke my heart. So now I'm just having sex. I've been married twice now but I don't get my heart all involved anymore, so to me it's always just sex."

Erica, thirty-something "I think making love is something you do with someone you are in love with, where you feel like you're one when you're together. You're connected. I think when you're having sex you care about that person and it feels good, but you know it's not going any further than that. You want him, and he wants you, but you understand that tomorrow he may be gone and if that's the case, then so be it."

Sadie, fifty-something "You make love with a man when you really love and care for him, and you want to give him the ultimate satisfaction, but sex can be altogether different."

"I've experienced making love, and I've experienced having sex. When I'm with my husband, I feel like I'm having sex just because he wants to and I feel like I have to fulfill an obligation. Once we're through I go to sleep, happy that it's over. When I'm with my lover, I feel like I'm making love because he does all he can to please me and vice-versa. When we finish, I always cry because I can't believe how good he makes me feel and I hate for it to be over.

"Me and my husband used to make love when we were younger, but as you get older, it changes. They start doing little things you don't like, or stop doing little things you do like. And of course the arguments over money, kids, and all this other little shit all falls right into the bedroom when you come down to it, so that changes the relationship and the sex."

Jill, thirty-something "Making love is not about pleasing yourself, it's about pleasing your mate while enjoying yourself at the same time. It's the ultimate fulfillment for two individuals who are deeply in love and sexually attracted to each other.

"Sex, on the other hand, is usually just sex."

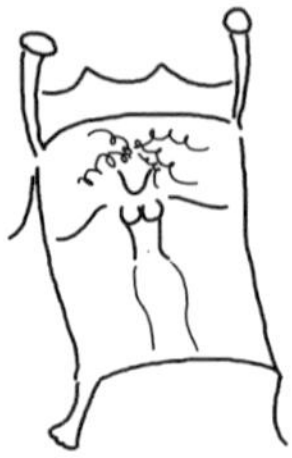

Oral/Anal

Kiana, forty-something "I think it's great to give and receive oral sex, but I'll always think receiving is so much better. I guess it's because that's when I have my most intense orgasms. There ain't nothing like it."

Celeste, fifty-something "I like it a lot, giving and receiving. My man is very good at performing oral sex, so I don't have to tell him what to do and that's nice. But I don't understand it when other women say, 'I would never kiss him afterwards.' Those are the most intimate kisses you'll ever have. If you know you're clean, what's the problem? If you're not, he shouldn't be down there in the first place."

India, thirty-something "You see, women look at their husbands and go, 'Uuuhhh . . . Suck his dick? I don't think so,' while at the same time another woman is looking at him and going, I love the ground he walks on and I'll suck his dick anytime.' I know because I'm doing it to somebody else's husband myself."

Nikki, fifty-something "I can take it or leave it, and I'm probably the worst at giving it because I'm not swallowing nothing. Shit, there ain't that much love in the world for me. When he feels like he can't hold back, it's time to either get a towel or change positions because I'd hate to have to get ugly and ruin the whole damn mood.

"Receiving is okay, but my body chemistry is weird. If it goes on too long, I get dry and end up with a yeast infection, so I'd rather not even do it. Now, if it's real quick, just to get the juices flowing so we can move on to the next thing, then I'm all right with it, but don't kiss me afterwards. Don't even put your lips on my face. I might not even want him to breathe on me because I don't want to smell or taste myself."

Erica, thirty-something "I think oral sex is wonderful if you know that person is clean. As long as you were there when he showered or you showered together and washed each other, then there shouldn't be a problem.

"I use oral sex as my opportunity to put on a show. Men like to watch, and I'd rather give than receive because some men don't really know how to hit the right spot anyway. It's not the ultimate for me, but if I'm with a man that I care very deeply for, I really enjoy making him feel good."

Bianca, thirty-something "I used to love oral sex until I dated a guy who had a big old gap in his teeth." Bianca closed her eyes and shook her head as she thought back. "I'd been dating him for about two months and finally decided to let him have some, and I told him we could skip the oral sex because I didn't really feel like I knew him well enough. But he insisted, saying I didn't have to go down on him, but he just had to taste it because the taste of a woman turned him on. Now you know when a man loves the way a woman tastes, he usually knows what he's doing because he's not inhibited.

"Well, let me tell you, the brother did know what he was doing, but he got carried away and my clitoris got caught in his gap—just for a second—and it hurt so bad that I got pissed off and told him to stop. Of course, he was upset because he wanted to finish what he'd started, but I dried up so there was no turning back. I told him to get his shit and leave and I never saw him again after that.

"Needless to say, I don't date men with gaps anymore."

Saundra, twenty-something "I enjoyed oral sex with my lover a lot. I could do it for hours because it turned him on so much. To me, it's just a normal part of making love. Unfortunately, he never reciprocated."

Miss Nora, sixty-something "Oh, no, honey. Miss Nora's not into that at all, and I'll tell them that straight from the beginning when they start talking about it. If they want to perform it on me, that's their business but don't ask me to return the favor. If I'm gonna make love, I'm gonna make love the old-fashioned way because I'm from the old school. Besides, I've had these dentures since high school, and I don't even like the way I look without them myself. I sure as hell don't intend to let a man see me without them in."

Jill, thirty-something "I like oral sex as long as I don't have to do it. Hey, I'm being honest. I'll receive it, but I don't want to give and I don't make that no secret. I've got a weak stomach. I don't like swallowing nothing slimy, and I gag too easily, so I don't even fool around when it comes to that."

Cheyanne, forty-something "Girl, I love oral sex, but let me tell you a really funny story. One time this guy I was seeing called and said he was on his way over and caught me off guard. He'd been out of town on business, so I wasn't expecting him back for a day or so. I'd just taken a bath, and a vinegar douche, so when he called I had to scramble to figure out what I was going to do because I didn't want him to taste that vinegar.

"Well, I'd gone to this little lingerie party about a month before and bought some of this stuff that looked like chips of ice that you were supposed to put in your mouth while performing oral sex on your partner. The girl who was selling the stuff said it could be used by men and women so I figured I'd use it on my man, and then get him to use it on me. I wanted him to think I was being freaky, but what I was really trying to do was camouflage that damn vinegar.

"As soon as he walked in, he was all over me. I said, 'Ooh, you missed me, huh? Well, hold on, baby. I've got a little treat for you. Why don't you go take your shower while I get it ready.' He was grinning from ear to ear as he headed for the bathroom. When he came out, I worked him over good with that ice or whatever that shit was called. He was moaning and moving around so much I had to tell him to be still before I lost my rhythm, but I was enjoying the hell out of making him lose control.

"Well, when it came time for him to use that stuff on me, I couldn't wait." Cheyanne looked at me with a smile forming at the corners of her mouth. "When he first got started, it was nice and cool, like chocolate ice cream in your mouth. But girl, about 30 seconds into it that shit mixed with that vinegar and I thought I was on fire! I was still trying to be sexy, whispering, 'Wait, baby, wait. Slow down. I'm not going nowhere,' but he wouldn't stop because he thought it was getting good to me. He grabbed my hips and held on like he was in a damn pie-eating contest because I was squirming, trying my best to get away from him. And . . . I can't believe you're laughing at me, girl."

"I'm sorry, Cheyanne," I said, still laughing, "but you know it's funny. I can't believe your little plan backfired. I'll bet you could have dug a hole and crawled in it, right?"

Cheyanne started to laugh herself. "Girl, you know I played it off. I told him I guess that stuff wasn't meant for men to use on women, and he believed me. Soon as he left I threw that shit in the trash and I've never tried anything like that again. I figure if a man catches me in a situation like that again, I'll just have to be honest with him and we can move on to something else."

Eboni, forty-something "Anal? You mean in the bootie? Oh, hell no, shit no, Eboni don't do that either. I got hemorrhoids. My tolerance level for pain is zero, and I don't want nothing back there that wasn't meant to go there. I can eat a hot sausage and that will mess me up for the next two days, so I don't fool around with that. If a man wants some from the ass, he needs to get a man. Hell, I'll even watch as long as it's going to keep me from doing it. I went to the hospital and had an enema one time, and I hope I never have to have another one of those. That was enough. I almost did it one time with my first husband. He said if we used Vaseline it wouldn't hurt, but I just couldn't get past the thought of it. I know a lot of people are into it, but not me."

Sadie, fifty-something Sadie paused before answering me when I asked her if she'd ever tried anal sex, and I immediately felt like I'd gone too far. Just when I was about to retract the question she said, "I've never tried it, and I don't want to because I know I wouldn't like it. I don't think I've ever loved a man enough to let him stick his penis in my butt. There are too many other ways to have sex that feel good. But I think anal sex would be way too painful, and I'm not into pain with sex, period. If it's hurting me, I ain't doing it, that's the bottom line."

She stopped again to sign some receipts and then waited until the waiter was out of hearing distance before speaking. "I had a friend who tried it, and she said it was very uncomfortable. I don't see how it can give women any pleasure because we don't have any moisture there and there's no stimulation for us. Besides, you can make your vagina just as tight as your ass if you know how.

"I had a lover who wanted me to experiment with anal sex one time and I politely told him, 'Let me put my legs on the inside and cross my ankles and that should feel tight enough for right now, but don't be asking me to do nothing crazy.' "

Shantay, thirty-something "I think if I could ever get over my fear of pain, I might like it. I tried it before, but I was almost knocked out with liquor so I really don't remember whether or not it was painful. Men like it because it feels so tight, but I think it's a mind thing with women. When you start thinking about doing that, your body just tightens up, and that's probably why so many women say it hurts so much. You've got to relax.

"I've heard that it helps to push as if you're forcing something out of your body until he gets in. Then once he's in, you can relax. I'd like to try it again, but it's not something I'd like to do on a regular basis."

Porsche, forty-something "I used to have anal sex all the time when I was in college," Porsche said, looking around like she thought someone might walk up behind her and hear. "I probably would have kept on doing it because I enjoyed it, but then when I was a medical intern, I saw a lady who was about to have surgery on her anus because it was so loose from having anal sex all the time, and that changed my mind.

"To me, it was a great feeling, something different, which is why the guys enjoy it. But it wasn't worth all that, so I gave it up."

Giovanni, forty-something "Oh Lord, I knew you were going to go there," Giovanni said, trying to look all innocent. "Yes, I tried it one time with my lover and to me it felt like I was trying to push something big out and he was trying to push it back in." She made a funny face, looking embarrassed. "I was very uncomfortable, but he was back there talking and shit, saying, 'Ooh, baby, that feels so good. You're so tight.' Shit, I guess his ass would be tight too if all he used it for was its intended purpose, which was exactly what I intended to keep using mine for once it was over. I only did it because he wanted to.

"That's probably why I can't get rid of his ass now. He thinks I'm going to let him do it again, but I've got news for him."

Saundra, twenty-something "Me and my boyfriend almost tried anal sex one time, but he didn't get all the way into it before he came. The circumstances we were under at that time would not have been comfortable anyway. It was like the spur of the moment, and there was no room to move around so that really wasn't the time. But I would like to experience it because it's something different. It seems like it would be exciting with the right person."

Kiana, forty-something "I have never been able to get into anal sex because it hurts. I've tried, I ain't gonna lie, but it did nothing for me. I used to work in a hospital and I've seen women who had anal sex regularly and their butt holes were huge. After doing that for so long you just lose all the elasticity."

Cassidy, forty-something "I ain't down with anal sex, girl. No. My husband used to ask me to do it all the time, but I'm not going there. He'd say, 'Cassidy, you're always willing to try something new. Why won't you at least just try it? As long as we've been together you know I'm not going to hurt you.' But you know how I broke him from asking me?

"I told him, 'I'll make a deal with you, baby. Let me go to the store and buy a dildo or a vibrator and when I get back, let me screw you in your ass first. Then you can screw me in mine.'

" 'Oh, hell no,' he said, looking at me like I was the one who was crazy. So, I don't have to worry about that shit no more because he knows I'm for real. That's how you break him. Turn the tables on his ass, and he won't ask you anymore. Not unless he's a freak for real."

ADVICE

ad-vice (ad-vis) noun
Recommendation regarding a decision.
Counsel.

Best Advice Received

Advice for Younger Women

Advice is something we've all received at one time or other. From the time we were children thinking about doing the things our parents told us not to do until the time we were adults doing things we knew we had no business doing.

What's some of the best advice you've ever received? Perhaps you never acted on it. Nine times out of ten you didn't. But it didn't take long to realize that the advice was sound, especially when you went and did the exact opposite.

How many times have you looked back over your life and wished you'd listened a little bit harder and minded a little bit more when your mama told you something? I don't think there's a person around that hasn't received at least one piece of good advice and wished they'd followed it. Well, that's what this chapter is all about. Enjoy!

"Work like you don't need the money.
Love like you've never been hurt.
Dance like nobody's watching."
—*Satchmo Paige*

"Advice is one of those things that is far more blessed
to give than to receive."
—*Carolyn Wells, 1937*

"I am very handy with my advice and then when anybody appears
to be following it, I get frantic!"
—*Flannery O'Conner, 1979*

"A woman in love never takes advice."
—*Rosamond Marshall, 1943*

"Advice is what we ask for when we already know
the answer but wish we didn't."
—*Erica Jong, 1977*

Best Advice Received

Giovanni, forty-something "Unfortunately, there aren't many ladies in this world anymore, at least as far as I can see from the way some women carry on—cussing up a storm, drinking like a sailor, or laughing and talking louder than any man in the room." Giovanni went to the small refrigerator located in the storeroom of her bookstore and brought out a bottle of Kendall-Jackson chardonnay. She also unearthed some very expensive looking wine glasses, uncorked the bottle, and began to pour. "I keep this stuff here for book signings and such. I also have some cheese and crackers. Would you like some?"

I declined, and then asked her how she'd learned to be so ladylike. "Not a day went by that my mama didn't tell me how important it was to look, act, walk, and talk like a lady, so it's a natural part of me, and I taught my girls the same thing." She sat down on one of the three plush sofas stationed around the store.

"I absolutely forbade my girls to call boys. And don't tell me how things are different today because they don't have to be. The rules have not changed when it comes to the fact that a man should treat a woman like a lady. I feel the same way about that now as I felt about it twenty years ago. If a man is thinking about you and wants to talk to you, then let him pick up the phone and call you.

"My brother, who is divorced and way too old to be dating by the way, told me that just yesterday in the span of two hours the same woman called his number twenty times, and he didn't bother to answer the phone because he just didn't feel like talking to her then. So, who's the fool? A man likes to be the one to do the chasing, so what's wrong with letting him? It's gotten so bad now that some men won't even take a woman out to dinner without expecting her to pay half, and if she doesn't pay half he's expecting sex. Now, why is that? Because women have allowed it, that's why. Women just don't seem to place much value on themselves anymore, and by value I'm not talking about how much she can get out of a man. I'm talking about respect." Giovanni leaned back on the sofa, crossed her legs, and held up her glass of wine. "Take a glass of wine, for instance. You've seen how some women will guzzle it down like Kool-Aid?" She shook her head in disgust. "A lady should always leave a few sips in the bottom of her glass."

I nodded my head in agreement, making a note to myself to remember not to drain my glass dry like I usually did. I like to believe I'm a lady, too, but there haven't been too many times when me or my girlfriends have left perfectly good wine sitting in a glass, especially when we were often the ones having to pay for it. I couldn't remember how many waitresses my good friend Tina had cussed out because they'd picked up her glass too soon when she still had one good sip left.

Giovanni didn't get in a hurry when she talked, either. She talked the same way she drank, slowly, like she was relishing the taste of her words. "My mama said that a woman should never try to measure arms with a man either because she'd lose every time." Giovanni could tell from the look on my face that I had no idea what she was talking about.

"A man can sleep with his wife's best friend and all his male friends will congratulate him on the conquest, while the women, when they find out, will shake their heads and say, 'That's a man for you.' But turn the tables for a moment and say that the wife decides to sleep with her husband's best friend. The conversation would be totally different. The men would think of her as easy and try to figure out how they could get some, too, and the women would label her a no-good, lying bitch who couldn't be trusted around their own men." Giovanni picked up her wine glass, took another small sip, and looked me dead in the eyes as she smiled slightly. "Did you ever notice how much more of an impact curse words have when the come from the mouth of a lady?"

Miss Nora, sixty-something

"My grandmama's name was Emily, but everybody called her Ms. Emma and I called her Mama. She raised me and always told me how important it was to get a good education. She'd always say, 'If you get a good education and put God first there is nothing you can't do.' Well, I didn't finish school like she wanted me to, but I still put God first in my life.

"Mama was able to send all her children to college and her only skill was in knowing how to sew. If she made you something, you could turn it inside out and wear it on both sides." Miss Nora pulled a handkerchief from her pocket. "See these stitches?" The stitches were so tiny you could barely see where one ended and the other began and as straight as any I'd seen done by machine. "Mama made this handkerchief a long, long time ago. It's one of the few things I have left that was hers, and it means a lot to me." Handling the cloth as if it were made of gold, she brought it to her nose and inhaled deeply, and you could tell by that simple act that she was picturing her grandmother all over again.

"She also taught me that a man should take care of his woman," Miss Nora said while peering over the top of her glasses and gazing at me sternly, as if somehow I'd failed to follow the rules. Surely she hadn't spotted me at that seafood restaurant last night when I pulled out my Visa card and paid for my boyfriend's dinner. But it was his birthday, I wanted to explain. I don't do that kind of thing all the time. He does stuff for me too. Maybe not as often, but he does. Then, like she was reading my mind, she went on to say, "I don't believe in giving men stuff. I was raised to believe that the man buys the food, the man buys the drinks, whatever." Yep, she'd definitely seen me last night, but I continued to play it cool.

"Look, baby, if he don't give you much when he's dating you, he's gonna give you even less when he marries you." She folded her handkerchief. "Now don't get me wrong; it works both ways. When my man got sick, I took care of him. I managed his checkbook, I paid his bills, I carried him to the doctor, and I got his medicine, but there ain't no way in the world I'm gonna let a big, strong, healthy man lay up in the house with me and do nothing except be there and then have the nerve to think I'm happy just because he's there.

"Mama was the same way, and she said time and time again, 'Ain't no man gon' come in here, lay in my bed, and eat my food if he ain't spending no money on me.' When Granddaddy started messing up with the money, she packed his clothes in a tin suitcase, took that suitcase out to the porch and threw it up in the air. When that suitcase hit the ground it burst wide open and his clothes went everywhere. Mama then turned around and looked right at me and said, 'If a nigga' care anything about you he'll do something for you.'" Miss Nora put the handkerchief back in her pocket, still reminiscing. "That was the best advice she ever gave me, and it's still good advice to this day."

Bianca, thirty-something

"Don't let nobody make a fool out of you." Bianca's face wore an expression that said she was not a woman to be messed with. No wonder men hesitated to come over and ask her for a dance whenever we went out. She was an attractive woman in her early thirties and was slowly coming to the realization that she might not ever get married.

She tucked a strand of hair behind her ear and lay her tortoise-rimmed shades on the bar. Staring at herself in the mirror that covered one wall of the bar, she checked to make sure that her makeup was still perfect, and it was.

"There was this one man in my life I was crazy about," she said. "There was nothing I wouldn't do for him. If he just happened to mention that he'd like a steak, when he got home a thick juicy T-bone would be coming hot off the grill along with a potato, green salad, and red wine. If he wanted to see his favorite team play basketball, I'd get tickets to the game and they'd be the best seats in the house. When his birthday came, I had a limousine take us to the most upscale restaurant and nightclub in town. And he still broke up with me. And you know why? He said I didn't need him. I had a good job, I had a nice house, I vacationed at places that most people only read about in books, so what could a man do for me? He wanted a woman who needed him."

Bianca swung around on the barstool and faced the dance floor where couples were grooving to Maxwell. One brother with a gold tooth winked at her. She scowled and quickly turned her stool the other way. "Shit. See? That's the kind of brother I get. I swear. Just last week I went to Harold's Barbecue in the old neighborhood and I guess the brother working inside called himself trying to flirt with me because he not only gave me an extra hotlink sandwich, he also threw in a bag of barbecue seasoning. He had a gold tooth too.

"Like I was saying, I don't get it. Wouldn't you think a man would want a woman who had something to bring to the relationship instead of one who can't keep a job, always walking around with her hands out, begging for shit? I ain't never wanted no sugar daddy. I just want somebody who I can love and who will love me in return."

Eboni, forty-something

Eboni looked as cool as a cucumber with her new short haircut. She'd lit a few candles earlier and the scent of eucalyptus was all over the room. She turned the jazz music down low so we could talk, but then her phone started to ring. When she didn't answer, the person on the other end wouldn't leave a message; they just hung up and called right back repeatedly. She finally gave in and answered it, snapped at him that she was too busy to talk, and told him, she'd call him later. Looking at her you'd never think she was well into her 40s because she had the figure of a woman twenty years younger. If she was wearing some kind of body shaper beneath that dress and it made her look that good, I was thinking, sign me up for one right now because it was doing one hell of a job. Only if you looked real closely could you see the fine lines etched across her forehead.

"If a woman's satisfied, she should never let her man know it. If he takes her shopping and spends $1,500 on whatever it is she wants, when they get home she still needs to ask him some shit like, 'Who in the hell was that bitch you were staring at in the mall?' They like it when you act jealous anyway, and believe me, if you're too gentle with a man, he'll mess over you every time.

"If I let a man stay at my house for a day or two and I say, 'Baby, I need some lunch money . . .' " she stuck her hand out, palm up, and I could actually picture some man pulling out his wallet and handing the whole thing over to her, ". . . I'm talking about at least $50 because the whole time he was staying with me, the lights were on, the air was on and the water was running. All those things add up to bills." Eboni gave an exasperated sigh. "It's amazing the things a woman will do just to say she's got a man. She'll let him drive her car, and she'll not only cook his dinner and wash his clothes, she'll buy the shit. My advice to a woman like that is, 'Stop acting so hard up. Men have been chasing women for years, but if you don't give them a chance to chase you because you're so eager, chances are you'll stay single.' "

Denise, thirty-something "I got pregnant at 17 and my mama and daddy told me one thing I'll always remember. They said, 'You're not the first and you won't be the last, so hold your head up high and keep on going.' "

Ruby, forty-something Ruby got up and started pacing again. "When I found out that my fiance had gotten another woman pregnant, I was this close to breaking up with him," she said and held her thumb and index finger an inch apart, "but my mama said to me, 'Baby girl, let me tell you something about life. That woman knew exactly what she was doing when she came up pregnant. She knew you'd leave him as soon as you found out. Now if you love that man the way you say you do, then keep him. Don't let her have the upper hand. I'm not saying he didn't make a very big mistake, but he loves you and you love him so stay with him and prove her wrong.' Believe it or not, that was very good advice because I've been with that same man now for 17 years. When his ex-girlfriend found out that I wasn't going to just toss him out of my life, she told him he had to take his son, so we did." Ruby stopped pacing, looked down at me, and shrugged. "Now I know that a lot of women wouldn't have done what I did. A lot of women would call me all kinds of a fool, but until you're in a situation, you don't know what you'd do."

Sadie, fifty-something "I'll give you some good advice all right," Sadie said as she poured more coffee in my cup without me asking. I know about relationships if I don't know nothing else because I've been married over half my life, and one thing I know for sure is that a woman should never put sex first in the relationship. When a woman puts sex first, it overpowers everything, especially her common sense, and you know some people don't even have common sense. That woman will end up blocking out the important things she needs in life just because some man is able to make her have an orgasm. I ought to know because I've done some stupid shit behind men who know how to make love." Sadie nibbled on a sandwich. "Sex has definitely got to be the last thing on your list.

"The questions you should be asking yourself are these: Is he a good provider? Is he willing to take care of you, not just financially but emotionally too? If you can answer yes to both of those questions then you're lucky because that kind of man doesn't come around very often. It's much easier to overlook mediocre sex than it is to overlook a man who treats you badly or is unable to provide for you and your children. It's easy to find a man who's good in bed, but that only takes you through to your next orgasm and if that's all he's good for, in the long run he ain't gonna do a damn thing for you."

Nikki, fifty-something "Remember your family because that's who you're always gonna have. You're gonna have that family if you don't have anything else. If there's a fire, you're gonna have that family; if there's a flood, you're gonna have that family; if there's fighting, when the fighting is over, you'll still be family."

Jazz, forty-something "When I was in high school my daddy told me, 'No matter what you want to be in life, be the best. If you want to be the town whore, be the best whore in town and you'll be respected for it.' That advice has always stuck with me, and I'll tell anybody, no matter what I do, even if I'm a nurse's aide cleaning shit, I'm going to be the best shit-cleaner you can find."

Porsche, forty-something "I've been on this earth well over thirty years now and I've finally realized that nobody can make you happy but you." Porsche twisted a braid around one finger, a habit she had when she was deep in thought. "A man can change into everything you thought you wanted him to be, but his changing won't make you happy and you can't waltz through life blaming your unhappiness on someone else's actions. I don't know how many years I've spent crying and saying to myself, 'I don't understand why I can't be happy, all I want is to be happy.' Well I've finally decided that nobody has any control over my happiness but me." I knew for a fact that she was right about that because I don't how many times a week some asshole pissed me off and had me carrying my bad attitude home like luggage.

"I've finally decided that if someone is making my life miserable, it's up to me to change things."

Bianca, thirty-something "The best advice I can give other women is don't be buying and doing everything for him when all he's done for you is tell you how good you look, if he's even taken the time to tell you that." Bianca frowned as she looked toward the entrance of the club. She was watching that door like Mr. Right was going to step through it any minute.

She turned away from the door and faced the bar again. "I learned my lesson. I cooked for his ass, bought him shit, gave him these thoughtful cards just to let him know I was thinking about him and you know what I got in return?" Bianca shredded a napkin between her fingers. "All I got was a hard dick and a broken heart."

"He didn't even give you a birthday card?" I asked.

"Hell, no," Bianca replied. "And something as simple as a card would've had me on cloud nine for days, but he didn't have a clue. So I finally got to thinking, if I don't even rate a birthday card, why am I wasting my time? I'd handed my heart over to him on a silver platter with a glass of champagne on the side, and he hadn't even noticed."

Bianca twisted back and forth on the barstool, bracing herself against the wrought iron railing at the bottom. "How can a man who can't help but know how much you care about him because you've made sure he knows it, think it doesn't matter that he can't even take the time to buy you a cheap ass birthday card? And hell, even if he don't care about me the way I care about him, the least he could do is pick me a flower every now and then. If he likes me enough to screw me, it's the least he can do."

Advice to Younger Women

Cassidy, forty-something "Stop running after men," Cassidy advised. "I just can't stand to see a woman running after a man. I had this one girlfriend who could not take no for an answer. The man had told her that he wasn't ready to settle down and get serious with anybody, didn't bother to return her phone calls, and when she did luck out and happen to catch up with him he acted like he wanted to be anywhere else except around her. He finally had to come right out and tell her that she just wasn't his type before she got the hint and left him alone.

"Don't put up with a man's shit just because you're afraid he'll leave you if you speak your mind. If you do that and he knows it, you better believe he's gonna start thinking, 'She's got to have me.' " Placing a hand on one hip she leaned toward me, trying to make sure I heard her. Of course the noise of the dryer forced her to talk louder than normal, which in turn caused half the beauty shop to tune in to her one-sided conversation. But it was quite obvious she didn't care one way or the other that she had an audience because she didn't bother to lower her voice.

"A man ain't a necessity like food or water. And don't even let me start talking about those women who complain about some woman stealing their man. Somebody please tell me . . . ." Cassidy put both hands together as if in prayer and raised her eyes heavenward. "Somebody please tell me how you can steal a grown man?" She clicked her tongue. "Nobody can tell me how because it ain't possible. There ain't no way in this world you gonna steal a man unless he wants to be stolen and believe me, if it was that easy, I'd be Mrs. Michael Jordan by now."

Veronica, thirty-something "I went to this women's retreat that my church held, but I only took the fun courses. I wasn't about to take some serious course that would scare me or make me think too hard. They were offering this one course on

Revelations. The book of Revelations scares me to death. I steered clear of that course and enrolled in one about the Other Woman and how she seduced your man. It was all based on the Bible. There are things in the Bible that surprise me. There's stuff about how ladies perfumed their sheets and covered their bodies with oils and powder. Women need to do those same types of things today. Now I know that sometimes we're too tired to even begin thinking about some oil or powder, but if your man likes a red light in the bedroom, buy a red lightbulb and screw it in. Your bedroom should be the best place in the house. The best place shouldn't be the living room or the kitchen. A lot of us use the bedroom to watch movies or sleep and leave sex as an afterthought.

"Before that retreat I hadn't bought new sheets in five years, but afterwards I went out and bought some silk ones and some Egyptian cotton ones. If you've never slept on a silk sheet, you definitely need to try it because it's very sexy.

"I also learned that a woman should dress to please her man. If he buys me a short, sexy nightgown that I really don't even want to see myself in, let alone somebody else, I dim the lights and wear it anyway. Don't worry about no cellulite, that poochie stomach, or the fact that your breasts are sagging a little. Wear that gown and wear it with an attitude, an attitude that makes him think that he's lucky to even get the opportunity to see you wearing something like that. And believe me, if he didn't want to see you in it, he wouldn't have bought it for you in the first place."

Veronica spied a couple at a table a few feet away from us, so into each other that the woman pouring the tea had to ask them twice if they wanted a refill since they hadn't even noticed her coming up beside their table. "Now those two look like they could be having an affair," Veronica whispered. "That's the way a married woman should treat her husband, like she's having an affair with him. Slap him on the butt sometimes, tell him how good he looks or smells, and most of all, keep your eyes open for the small things, the little things that don't add up. You know what I'm talking about. If you can't do nothing to please him, then something's wrong. If the only time he seems to be halfway satisfied is when you're in bed making love, something's wrong. And when he starts picking at every little thing, asking 'Why you doing this . . . . I don't like the way you're wearing your hair . . . . You need to lose some weight,' you need to sit up and take notice because he's trying to tell you something important. There's something going on that's much deeper than a hairstyle or a few extra pounds.

"I didn't realize that all those hints meant something until I found out my husband was cheating on me with my best friend. A woman needs to take care of herself, and by that I don't mean she needs to concentrate on getting her hair done or her nails polished, even though that's all well and good. But she also needs to hit the gym a few times a week or find a track and go walking every other day. Remember that whatever it took to get him will be the same thing it takes to keep him."

Sadie, fifty-something "These girls need to let these boys know they want to be treated with respect," Sadie stated firmly. "If a boy isn't willing to respect a girl, he needs to move on. I'm a true believer that if you don't have your self-respect, you don't have nothing.

"There are a lot of young girls and grown women who give their bodies away as if it doesn't mean anything, and that's unfortunate. If a girl wants a boy to respect her, she needs to respect herself. She needs to stand out from the others and be different.

"Men were made to be conquerors, so let them do the chasing. I tell young women all the time, if a man has ten women chasing behind him and you're the only one who's not, you're going to get his attention."

Louise, sixty-something "Don't start off doing nothing you don't plan to keep on doing because the way you start out is the way it's gonna be. A man goes into a relationship expecting the woman to stay the same, while a woman goes into a relationship expecting the man to change. If you're giving him head every night and then decide you don't want to do it no more, there's gonna be a problem. If you draw his bath water every evening and then one day stop because you're tired of doing it, there's gonna be a problem. What difference does it make that you have two children now? Who cares that you're too tired to do anything more than brush your teeth and go to bed after you've seen to all the other shit like folding clothes and washing dishes? All he's gonna care about is the fact that you stopped doing what you used to do and wonder why you changed."

Miss Nora, sixty-something Miss Nora was always one to give out free advice, whether the person she was advising wanted to hear it or not. She was just like my mama, forever telling you some shit you don't want to hear about, especially when you know she's telling you the truth.

"Now I know about men, and a woman needs to be careful when a man starts asking her about where she works and what kind of car she drives," Miss Nora said. "He don't need to know nothing about all that unless he's trying to be a bo-weavel. You do know what a bo-weavel is, don't you? A bo-weavel is an animal who's always looking for a home and somebody to take care of him." Miss Nora crossed her legs and kept on talking, aware that my ears had perked and that I was nodding my head in agreement. She was in her element.

"I never let that happen to me. I wasn't no young fool, and I sure ain't gonna be no old one. If you went in there right now and looked in my bedroom you could see that I sleep on one side of the bed and I got my Bible, newspapers, and bills on the other." She clicked her tongue. "Ain't no man just gon' come in my house, lay up in my bed, or eat at my table without contributing nothing. If I'm seeing a man, he's gonna have to spend some money on me. I ain't talking about taking his whole paycheck, but at the very least take me out to dinner before you even think about taking me to bed.

"It's not that I can't cook. I just cooked some cornbread and a big pot of mustard greens this morning—six bunches and they taste damn good, but a woman should never allow herself to be used. Yeah, I got a house and I got a bed, but if he wants to sleep with me, he needs to spend his money. Don't try to use what I already got. I don't mind standing up on my feet for hours and cooking for him, but if he wants me to cook, we need to go to the grocery store so he can buy whatever it is he wants to eat. And I'm not gonna cook for him too many times if he don't put some money in my hand. You got to have money for almost everything. You can't do nothing without it."

Kat, thirty-something "My mom used tell me all the time, 'Life is not a fairy tale.' Kat wiped off the lipstick she was testing and reached for another shade. She was totally ignoring the man at the next table who was staring at her like he'd never seen a woman so beautiful.

"I didn't believe her then, but I do now," she continued. "Wisdom definitely comes with age. You have to work hard to make a relationship work because it just doesn't happen all by itself.

"I'd always fantasized that my marriage was gonna be this wonderful Cinderella/Snow White/Prince Charming thing but it's nothing like that. Mothers should make it a point to tell their daughters that life is not always going to be Disney World, and sex isn't always gonna be fireworks and shooting stars. I'd always looked forward to being swept off my feet like that woman in the movie *An Officer and a Gentleman*. Remember the part at the end of the movie where he comes striding into the place where she works, sweeps her off her feet, and rides off into the sunset with her to live happily ever after? That's what I imagined because that's all I saw. I never thought about what happened to Cinderella and Prince Charming after they'd lived together for a few years and had a couple of children. I think that's why women get so frustrated after being married a few years. They don't try to see past the sweeping-off-the-feet part in the beginning. All of that shit changes after four or five years, when you've gained five or ten pounds and he couldn't sweep you off your feet if he tried."

Eboni, forty-something "Why does a woman always try to change a man?" Eboni asked. "The reason so many women lose sleep behind a man is because they are laying up wide awake trying to figure out how to make him change.

"And what's the first thing a woman will cut off when she calls herself trying to punish a man?" I knew the answer before she even said it. "She'll start rationing her coochie out to him like it was some kind of endangered species, like he couldn't get it from somebody else if he wanted to." The phone started to ring again and this time Eboni looked at the caller ID and ignored it. It was clear that she was still bitter about her divorce, but apparently she hadn't had a problem getting a new boyfriend. Men had always been crazy about her. "Withholding sex is not the answer. What a woman needs to do is just take him the way he is or move on to somebody else."

Kat, thirty-something Kat always appeared self-confident to me, so I was surprised when I heard her say how afraid she used to be to let a man know how she really felt about anything because it might push him away. She broke a teacake in half and brushed the crumbs off the tabletop.

"A woman should put her happiness before anything else, and she should never be afraid to let a man know how she feels. If he wants to have sex in the park but you'd feel more comfortable in a hotel, tell him. If you don't tell him and you go ahead and have sex in the park, jumping at every strange sound, he's gonna think you're okay with it. If you think your honesty will run him off, you don't need him. If he leaves you because of your honesty, he was going to leave you anyway. You shouldn't have to bite your tongue or get all stressed out because you're afraid to let your feelings show. Stop hoping and praying that shit will change and he'll suddenly wake up one day so totally in love with you he can't see straight. It's never gonna happen that way."

Porsche, forty-something

Porsche sneaked a bite of my chicken salad, hummed and closed her eyes tightly like it was the best thing she'd ever tasted. It was pretty good. You can't go wrong with grilled chicken breasts, fresh squeezed lemon juice, walnuts, olive oil, and mayonnaise.

Porsche swallowed, then took a long swig of bottled water. "I hope you don't mind me eating while we talk, but this salad is the shit, girl. Okay, let's see, what kind of advice would I give to a young lady?" She thought about it for a few seconds. "I'd tell her to never put all of her eggs in one basket. Women have this tendency to go into marriage or a relationship with a mentality of 'This will last forever. I'm so happy. My husband would never leave me.' I mean, it's fine if she wants to think positively, but she still needs to be realistic. She still needs to take care of business.

"A woman should always put something aside for herself; I don't care if it's just five dollars a week. If saving that five dollars a week means not buying that Blue Bell Homemade Vanilla ice cream on your grocery list then that's what you need to do, because, believe me baby, when a man decides to leave, he leaves." Porsche took another bite of salad and chewed thoughtfully.

"I've personally witnessed three divorces of close girlfriends. All were middle aged and not one of them had put anything aside for a rainy day. One woman had to sell her house and move into an apartment because she couldn't afford the house note. Her alimony payments didn't even come close to covering the mortgage. This woman hadn't worked a day in her married life. She had a master's degree in business administration, but when they got married she decided to quit her job and stay at home and be his wife. That was her job. He handled everything else. He left her when their youngest child was a senior in high school."

Porsche reached for a few of the purple grapes that I had brought along. "I would tell a young woman that she should never give up herself so completely. Sure, it's nice to be somebody's wife, but that doesn't mean she has to become a complete extension of that man. She should be able to say, 'Hey, I love you with all my heart and soul, but if you feel like you need to go I'll fix you a lunch because I don't want you to go hungry.' "

Miss Charsie, fifty-something "The advice I'd give to any woman is that she should test a man to see if he really cares about her. Start asking him for things. If she asks him three times and he still hasn't given her anything or he always has an excuse for why he can't, then she needs to let his ass go because it's clear he ain't about nothing but the sex. If he can't give her some little thing that might cost $10 dollars or he can't find the time to take her somewhere when she needs a ride, but then he can turn around and ask for a blowjob, he ain't worth it.

"My daughter met this guy and they had been talking off and on by phone for about two weeks, and you know what he asked her? He said, 'I been talkin' to you for two weeks, tryin' to get to know you and stuff. When I'm gon' get to know the cat?' She hung up in his face and when he had the nerve to call back, she told him not to call her anymore because he couldn't do anything for her if that was all he wanted. She'd already seen what happened to her other girlfriends when they slept with a boy too soon.

"Then there's the situation with my niece, who would meet a boy one day and be in bed with him the next. A woman should not take her body and sex so lightly. Now how long you think a boy's gonna stay with a girl that gives it up that quickly? You'd think she would've figured this shit out by now. It's not like it's rocket science or anything because it happens over and over again. Unfortunately, she grew up in a family where her mother and some of her aunts went from man to man. So, if that's all she had for role models then what was she supposed to do? She was fighting an uphill battle anyway. She wasn't taught any better, so that's all she knows."

From the Authors—a final note of advice:

Life is short, and tomorrow is not promised to anyone, so we must make the best of each day. The gumbo of your life can be full of laughter, fun, and happiness, or sadness and disappointment; it's all in what you choose. Each of us has a spirit within: a light that will shine to show us the path we should take. But only when we stop trying to find our happiness in a man, or a new hairdo, or dress, and look within will we find that light. We often short-change ourselves when looking too hard to find what we already have, and that's our God-given gift of wisdom and discernment.

> Isaiah 30:21 says: "Whether you turn to the right or to the left, your ears will hear a voice behind you saying, 'This is the way, walk in it.' " If you simply ask and are willing to listen, that voice will always tell you the right way to go.

In closing . . .

We hope you enjoyed the read. Did you find yourself in any of these stories? Did you reminisce about some of your own escapades and find yourself smiling or maybe even feeling sad? Well, happy or sad, it's always good to know you're not alone when facing the things that life throws your way. It's good to be able to nod your head in agreement and think, "Girl, I know exactly where you're coming from." And the sex . . . the toe-curling, make-you-wanna'-holla' sex . . . isn't it good to know that chemistry like that doesn't exist just in romance novels?

Do you plan to take some of the advice you've read and pass it on to another sister who's struggling with a situation similar to yours? If so, our mission has been accomplished. We just want you to know that you're not alone, no matter what you might be going through. No matter what you might be facing, you can best believe that some other woman has faced that same thing. And guess what? They survived.

Always remember, your gumbo or your life is what you make it. Even though you may put in too much of one thing or not enough of the other, rest assured, in the end it will all come out fine.

Please write us with your comments regarding *Sister Gumbo—Life, Sex and More Sex*. We look forward to hearing from you. You can reach us at www.SisterGumbo.com or write to Sister Gumbo, P.O. Box 19252, Fort Worth TX 76119, or call 1-866-77GUMBO (774-8626)

We are currently at work on our next book, Sister Gumbo from the male point of view. Maybe you can let us know what it is you want to hear from the men. It's gonna be interesting!

Thanks for picking up *Sister Gumbo—Life, Sex, and More Sex*.

Be blessed.

Sincerely,

Ursula Inga Kindred and Mirranda Guerin-Williams

Sister Gumbo is the work of two sisters, originally from Baton Rouge, Louisiana, who are lucky enough to be able to talk to each other and their friends about anything. No subject is taboo. Throughout all the listening and talking, it finally occurred to them that women shared a lot of similar life experiences.

Both are voracious readers who realized that bookstores and library shelves were missing fun-filled, enjoyable books that all women could relate to. They decided to write ***Sister Gumbo*** to give readers a book that was a pleasure to read and not peppered with words you had to look up in a dictionary to understand—a book where the reader could point to a paragraph, nod her head and say, "Girl, I've been there."

Ursula Inga Kindred has a bachelor of business administration degree in finance, from Texas Christian University. She is employed as a senior cost analyst for a large aeronautics company, and has future aspirations of becoming a full-time author. She lives outside of Fort Worth, Texas in the country with her husband, Wade, and their two sons.

Mirranda Guerin-Williams spent six years in the U.S. Air Force; worked as a licensed cosmetologist; and is now employed by the federal government. She is pursuing a bachelor's degree in sociology, after which she plans to become a speaker and counselor for teens and engaged couples. She resides in a small town just outside of Fort Worth, Texas with her husband, Jerome, and their daughter and son.